W9-DBS-863

OUTBACK BOSS, CITY BRIDE

OUTBACK BOSS, CITY BRIDE

BY

JESSICA HART

MILLS & BOON®
Pure reading pleasure

For Stella and Julia, my City Screen plotting team

CHAPTER ONE

'THAT'S the man you want.'

Meredith's dubious gaze followed the pointing finger across the road to where a grim-looking man was just getting out of a battered truck. Not your typical Australian, was her first thought. He was very dark, for a start, and while everyone else out here seemed to radiate a kind of laconic good humour, his face was set in severe, almost intimidating, lines.

As she watched from her vantage point on the pub veranda, he jammed a hat on his head and slammed the truck door. He looked as if he were in a very bad mood.

'Are you sure?' she asked doubtfully.

'Course I'm sure.' Bill, owner of the pub and self-appointed guide to Whyman's Creek, hoisted his trousers up over a substantial stomach. 'I know everyone round here,' he pointed out proudly. 'We don't get many strangers passing through.'

Meredith could believe it. Whyman's Creek appeared to consist of a pub, a store, an airstrip and not much else. There were a few houses set in dusty, treeless yards dominated by water tanks and a road that ran straight through the town— if you could call it a town—its tarmac wavering in the brutal heat.

And that was it. Meredith knew, because she had explored every inch of it. She had been in Whyman's Creek for eighteen hours, and that was seventeen and a quarter hours too many in her book.

'This guy works at Wirrindago, does he?' she asked Bill as the man turned towards the store.

'He does more than work there. He owns it,' said Bill. 'All one thousand square kilometres of it.'

Meredith tried to imagine a thousand square kilometres, but couldn't do it. Not that it mattered; she had got the point. Wirrindago was a lot bigger than the backyard of her tiny terraced house in London. You'd think if you owned all that land you'd look a bit happier, she thought, eyeing Hal Granger critically.

Still, she didn't need him to tell jokes. She just needed him to take her to Lucy.

'Thanks, Bill,' she said. 'I'll go and have a word with him.'

But before she could decide how she was going to approach him, Bill had put his fingers in his mouth and produced a piercing whistle that made her flinch. 'Hal!' he called. 'Over here, mate!'

The man called Hal stopped with a hand on the screen door of the store and Meredith could feel his exasperation from the other side of the road. 'What is it, Bill?' he demanded irritably.

Not at all put out by the ungracious response, Bill beamed and pointed at Meredith with his thumb. 'Young lady here wants you,' he shouted back, not that there was any need to raise his voice, Meredith reflected. There wasn't exactly a deafening roar of traffic.

Meredith couldn't actually hear Hal's sigh, but it might as well have boomed out over the outback as he turned and headed across the road. He stopped at the bottom of the steps leading up to the pub's veranda and frowned up at her, just in case he wasn't looking intimidating enough already.

'Yes?' he said.

'I'll leave you two to it,' said Bill comfortably. 'Hal'll see you right,' he added to Meredith, blissfully unaware of Hal's obvious irritation, or perhaps too familiar with his scowl to notice. With a final hoist of his trousers, he disappeared into the gloom of the pub, leaving Hal and Meredith regarding each other.

Neither was impressed.

Meredith felt at a distinct disadvantage. It was perfectly obvious that Hal Granger was in no mood to grant favours. Beneath his hat, his eyes were a startlingly light grey and very cold and the dark, frowning brows did nothing to alleviate the impression of barely leashed temper she had sensed when she'd watched him get out of the truck. With that fierce scowl, beaky nose and stern mouth, he could hardly be called a good-looking man, but there was no denying the force of his personality.

Hal Granger, she guessed, was someone to be handled with care. It would have been much better if she had gone over and introduced herself, rather than let Bill whistle him over like a dog.

On the other hand, at least he was there. She couldn't do anything about it now, and if she dithered any longer about the best way to approach him, he would get even more cross. Putting on her best smile, Meredith took off her sunglasses, with the vague idea that it might make her seem friendlier and more approachable, although not wearing them didn't seem to have that effect on Hal Granger.

'I'm so sorry to interrupt you,' she began, absurdly conscious of her English vowels. She had never realised that she sounded so like the Queen before. 'But Bill was telling me that you own a cattle station called Wirrindago.'

Hal ignored his cue to ask her what he could do for her. 'Yes,' he said again unhelpfully.

Meredith kept her smile fixed in place and ploughed on. 'I'm Meredith West. I believe my sister's working for you…Lucy,' she prompted and the strange light eyes narrowed slightly.

'Yes, Lucy's at Wirrindago. I'd forgotten that her surname was West,' he admitted.

'Is she OK?' asked Meredith anxiously.

'She was fine when I left this morning.'

'Oh, thank goodness for that!' Meredith's shoulders slumped in relief.

In spite of Bill's assurances that Lucy often

came into town on Saturday night with the Wirrindago stockmen and was, according to him, the life and soul of the party, she hadn't been able to help thinking of all sorts of horrible reasons why her sister hadn't been in touch. Lucy was sick, had been kidnapped, had an accident, lost her memory, been taken over by aliens...Meredith had run through all the possibilities countless times and the longer she didn't hear from Lucy, the more plausible they all seemed.

Something about Hal Granger's cool indifference reassured her in a way that Bill's friendly concern hadn't been able to and Meredith could relax at last.

For as long as it took her to wonder why, if Lucy really *was* OK, her sister hadn't been in touch. Surely Lucy wasn't still feeling awkward about the way they had parted? Meredith fiddled anxiously with the arm of her sunglasses.

Hal watched relief warring with worry in her face as she gnawed uncertainly at her lip. It was rather a nice lip too, he was annoyed with himself for noticing. She had a soft, generous mouth that sat oddly with sharp intelligence in her eyes and a certain briskness in her expression.

He would never have guessed that she and Lucy were related. Lucy was blonde and slender and lovely. Her sister was darker, with a round, curvaceous figure and brown hair that looked as if it had been ruthlessly cut to restrain any tendency to unruly curls.

Hal wouldn't have said that she was pretty—not exactly—but even to his inexpert eye she was immaculately groomed. She had on a pair of well-cut trousers and a tailored pale blue shirt that she wore with a string of pearls—*pearls,* for God's sake!—and her shoes had little peep toes so that he could see her painted toenails from his vantage point at the bottom of the steps.

She looked cool and capable and utterly ridiculous. If she were holding up a card screaming 'city girl' in glaring letters, she could hardly have made it clearer that she was completely out of place.

Hal had no time for city girls.

He settled his hat on his head. 'Is that it?' he asked.

Meredith's head jerked up at that and she

stared at him. Her eyes, Hal realised with an odd jolt, were a deep, dark blue and very beautiful.

'I'd hardly have come all the way out from England to ask one question, would I?' she said tartly before she could stop herself. 'Of course that's not it!'

Hearing the irritation in her voice too late, Meredith made herself stop and draw a breath. She had to ask him a favour and she wasn't going the right way about it, but honestly! It must be perfectly obvious she needed more than to hear that Lucy was OK.

She had been travelling for what seemed like days and she was hot and worried and woozy with jetlag. Why couldn't he just be nice and offer to take her to Lucy, preferably on a magic carpet that would transport her there in an instant because if she had to travel an *inch* more she was going to crumple into a heap and cry with exhaustion?

But crumpling wasn't an option and nor was crying. It never was, in Meredith's experience, although other people she knew seemed to get away with both on plenty of occasions.

So she straightened her shoulders, folded her

sunglasses and pinned what she hoped was a conciliatory smile on her face.

'The thing is, I need to see Lucy,' she said. 'I'd hoped to hire a car to get me to Wirrindago, but Bill tells me that's not practical.'

'It's more than not practical. It's irresponsible and stupid,' said Hal flatly. 'You weren't seriously planning to set off on your own into the bush?'

'I presume there are roads,' said Meredith, hating the fact that she sounded defensive.

'Not the kind of roads *you're* used to,' he said. 'There aren't a lot of signs either. You wouldn't last five minutes.'

Meredith stiffened. If there was one thing she hated, it was being told that she couldn't do something, but she folded her lips on a snappy retort just in time. She couldn't afford to alienate him any more than she had apparently done just by standing there, or she would be stuck here in Whyman's Creek, and that was the last thing she wanted.

'No, well, that's more or less what Bill said,' she conceded. 'Which is why I need your help.' She drew a breath. 'I was wondering if you could take me with you when you go back to Wirrindago.'

'*You* want to come to Wirrindago?' His hard grey gaze swept dismissively over her and Meredith stiffened. There was no need for him to make it quite that clear what he thought of her. 'I don't think it's your kind of place,' he said.

'I don't think it's likely to be my kind of place either,' she retorted sharply, given that conciliation didn't seem to be getting her anywhere. 'That's not the point. The point is that I need to talk to my sister, and unless I want to hang around here until the weekend on the off-chance that she'll come in to town, I'll just have to get myself there, and you seem to be my best chance.'

She stared down at him with angry blue eyes. 'I'll pay for petrol if it helps,' she told him, and Hal's black brows drew even closer together at the thinly veiled contempt in her voice.

'There's no question of payment,' he snapped. 'Of course I'll take you back with me, since you insist, but you're going to have to wait. I've got several jobs to do while I'm here.'

'Perhaps I could help you?' suggested Meredith, not much liking the idea of yet more waiting. She had been hanging around Whyman's Creek long enough. 'Jobs are usually quicker with two,' she pointed out. 'If you've got a list, I could do your shopping, or—'

'I don't think so.' Hal cut her off.

He could think of nothing worse than trying to get through everything he had to do with this woman trotting along beside him in her stupid shoes and no doubt trying to organise him with that English voice. She looked the bossy type, and Hal didn't like bossy women any more than he liked city girls.

'You stay here,' he ordered. 'I'll come and get you when I've finished.'

'Well, then, could we arrange a time for you to pick me up?' suggested Meredith, who liked to have a plan.

'No, we couldn't,' said Hal as he turned to go. 'If you want to come back to Wirrindago with me, you're just going to have to wait.'

Charming.

Huffily, Meredith watched him stride off. It wouldn't have killed him to give her some indication of how long he was going to be, would it?

She turned back to the veranda with a sigh. It looked like being a long wait.

And it was. Meredith couldn't believe how one

man could contrive to spend so much time in Whyman's Creek. Five minutes had been enough for her, but Hal Granger seemed capable of keeping himself busy there for hours.

It felt like hours anyway.

Anxious in case he forgot about her, Meredith brought out her suitcase and stayed on the pub veranda to keep a vigilant watch on the street. It wasn't hard to follow him as he moved between the store and the bank and what Bill had told her was the stock agent's office. Whyman's Creek wasn't the kind of town where crowds thronged the streets. In fact, sometimes Hal Granger was the only person in sight and Meredith was sure he was deliberately taking his time to keep her waiting.

Irritably, she waved the flies from her face. It was incredibly hot, even in the shade, and she wanted nothing more than to lie down somewhere cool and go to sleep for a week. In spite of the discomfort, her eyelids kept closing and she had to jerk herself awake. The moment she fell asleep she knew Hal Granger would have driven off to Wirrindago without her, claiming that she 'wasn't ready'.

So she took out her laptop and tried to concentrate on some work, but it was hard when Hal's tall, austere figure kept catching at the corner of her eye as he crossed the street or came out of the store, and his grim features seemed to shimmer between her eyes and the computer screen. Those pale, almost silvery eyes were definitely striking and while Meredith didn't think that she had noticed the angular planes of his face or the set of his mouth particularly, it was amazing how clearly she could picture them now.

Amazing and more than a little disturbing.

She had managed to download her emails in Brisbane the night before, but she was so tired that the words blurred on the screen and she was very close to dozing off in spite of everything when Hal came out of the store opposite and got into the truck.

Jerking upright, Meredith got ready to run after him, but it turned out that he hadn't forgotten her after all. He threw the truck into a wide U-turn and stopped at the bottom of the pub steps.

Hastily, Meredith shoved her laptop into its case and reached for her suitcase but, to her surprise, Hal Granger was already there.

'I'll take it,' he said abruptly.

'Really, I can manage perf—' she began, but he ignored her, carrying the case down the steps and tossing it into the back of the truck with insulting ease.

'—fectly well,' Meredith finished under her breath as she followed him. She had already taken a fond farewell of Bill, who was delighted to hear that she expected to be back again very soon. She would be back with Lucy or she would be on her own, but either way she didn't intend to spend any longer in the outback than she had to.

'Do you want me to take that?' Hal nodded at her laptop.

Meredith eyed the back of the truck askance, where her suitcase sat in a thick layer of dust between a couple of sealed boxes and a jumbled collection of farm machinery. At least, she guessed it was farm machinery.

There was no way she was putting her precious laptop in there.

'I'll keep it with me, thanks,' she said, clutching it protectively to her chest as if afraid that Hal would wrest it from her.

He shrugged. 'Suit yourself,' he said, opening his door.

Meredith hurried round to the other side and clambered awkwardly up into the cab, where there seemed to be just as much dirt as in the back. Fastidiously she brushed at the seat but it didn't seem to make much difference and she suppressed a sigh as she sat down and searched around her for a seat belt. Her trousers were going to be ruined.

'Sorry about the dust,' said Hal, not sounding particularly sorry. 'The air-conditioning's broken.'

Great. Meredith's heart sank. So much for her magic carpet, she thought, brushing at her trousers in a futile attempt to clean them. It looked like being an uncomfortable journey.

Not that that would probably bother Hal Granger. Comfort didn't seem to be very high on his agenda. The truck was basic, to say the least. Meredith was used to cars with comfortable bucket seats separated by a gear stick. Here, the gear shift was set oddly in the steering wheel column and the seat was a single hard bench, its plastic covering torn in places and oozing some mean brownish foam.

Still, perhaps she was lucky there was any padding at all, Meredith reflected. She'd thought bench seats like this went out in the Sixties before seat belts were enforced. Weren't these the kind of car seats just made for making out on? Not that she had ever been the kind of girl who was taken out for a date that ended in a clinch in some secluded parking spot, but she'd read plenty of novels where teenagers got carried away and took advantage of the lack of obstructions to get horizontal.

Meredith sighed. Typical that her only experience of turbulent teenage passion was through books.

Or of roaring-towards-thirty-verging-on-middle-age-if-she-wasn't-careful passion, come to that.

She glanced at Hal Granger as he put the truck into gear and wondered if he had ever put the bench seat to good use. He must have been a teenager once, although it was hard to imagine now that he was all grim, solid man and, anyway, where would he have found a heavy date living out here in the middle of nowhere?

Presumably people *did* meet and marry, though. Hal might even be married himself. It was a thought that made Meredith pause. *Was* he married? He was a few years older than her—

pushing forty, she guessed—so it wasn't beyond the bounds of possibility, although she couldn't quite picture it, somehow. He seemed so closed and stern, it was impossible to think of him happy and smiling, falling in love, *making* love…

Which was a shame, really, with a mouth like that.

The thought came out of nowhere, like an unexpected poke in the stomach, and Meredith was so shocked by it that she actually gasped. It was little more than an indrawn breath, in fact, but the next instant she found herself skewered by Hal's cold, oddly light, grey gaze as he turned his head to look directly at her.

'Are you OK?' he asked, frowning, his hand stilling on the gear shift.

To her horror, Meredith found herself blushing. 'Yes, fine,' she said quickly. 'I'm just…a bit hot, that's all.'

Oh, God, what had she said *that* for? She had made it sound faintly suggestive, and if it had seemed like that to her, what would Hal have made of it?

'I'm fine,' she added again, ridiculously flustered.

To her intense relief, Hal didn't seem to notice anything amiss. 'There'll be a bit of a breeze once we get going,' he said.

'A bit of a breeze', Meredith discovered as they bowled along the tarmac, was his way of describing the constant buffeting of the air through the open windows. In no time at all it had snarled her hair into an impenetrable tangled mess and deposited what felt like an inch-thick layer of red dust on her face. When she lifted her hand to touch her cheek it felt like sandpaper and she grimaced.

'How long will it take us to get to Wirrindago?' she asked, raising her voice above the sound of the rushing air.

Hal shrugged. 'Couple of hours,' he suggested.

'A couple of *hours*?' Appalled, Meredith stared at the tarmac, stretching remorselessly straight ahead until it vanished into the shimmering heat haze. 'I didn't realise it would take so long,' she confessed.

'Two hours is a good trip.' He glanced at her as she struggled to keep her dark hair from blowing about her face. 'It can take a lot longer in the Wet when there's water in the creeks,' he told her. 'Sometimes we can't get across at all and have to fly in and out.'

'It seems a long way to go for some shopping,' Meredith commented, thinking longingly of the supermarket just round the corner from her London house. That was a three minute walk, max. 'Isn't there anywhere closer?'

'No,' said Hal. 'Whyman's Creek is as local as it gets. We don't come in unless we absolutely have to.'

'I can see why,' said Meredith. She couldn't imagine why anyone would want to go to Whyman's Creek if they could possibly avoid it. Bill had made it sound as if a trip into town was a regular Saturday night jaunt for the stockmen at Wirrindago, but what on earth did they do when they were there? There was nothing to see, nothing to do, just the crushing heat and the flies and the fine red dust that seemed to settle over everything.

Presumably the pub was the draw, although its appeal was rather lost on Meredith.

One thing, she surely wouldn't have any problems persuading Lucy to leave with her, Meredith consoled herself. If anything could have cured her sister of her romantic ideals, it would have to be working for a man like Hal Granger in this awful, empty place.

'The outback's beautiful,' Lucy had raved. 'I can't wait to get out there and find some real men! Outback men, Lucy had assured her sceptical elder sister, were universally strong and silent. They rode horses and wore hats and checked shirts, and they were all slow quiet charm and rangy grace.

Meredith's mouth quirked as she glanced sideways at Hal Granger. He was rangy, yes, and he had a hat, she'd give him that, but he was clearly short in the charm and grace department. Of course, he might look different if he smiled, she conceded to herself, but he didn't look as if he did that very often. He might smile at Lucy though, Meredith reminded herself. Men usually did.

Not that Lucy was likely to be impressed if he drove this clapped-out truck instead of riding a wild stallion. He didn't even have the decency to wear a checked shirt. Poor Lucy's illusions must have been shattered, thought Meredith, amused. If she were Lucy, she would leap at the chance to escape.

But if she were Lucy, she would be the one Richard wanted to see and she wouldn't be here at all.

Meredith's smile faded at the thought of Richard. She wished she knew how he was. She hadn't been able to get a signal to call his mother that morning. It seemed weeks since she had stood by that hospital bed and promised to find Lucy, but it couldn't have been more than two—three?—days ago. Tiredly, Meredith wiped the dust from her cheek with the flat of her hand. She had been through so many time zones she had lost track of the days completely.

Hal heard her sigh and glanced at her. She looked tired, he thought with a touch of compunction. Judging by the pallor of her skin, she was fresh off the plane from London and she was probably exhausted.

He should have been more helpful, he thought. He wasn't normally that ungracious. It was unfortunate that she'd got him on a bad day.

Everything seemed to be going wrong recently. Someone only had to look at a piece of machinery for it to break at the moment. They hadn't had enough rain. Fences were down and bank charges up, and on top of that he had the kids to deal with…Meredith's glossy assurance as she'd stood at the top of the pub steps, literally looking down on him, had caught him on the raw. At first glance, she had seemed to represent everything that Hal least liked and least trusted.

But she wasn't complaining, he noticed with grudging respect, even though she was obviously not enjoying herself. Her mouth—that surprisingly lush mouth that didn't seem to go at all with the astringency of her personality—was turned down at the corners as she surveyed the road ahead, evidently profoundly unimpressed by the road that cut across the vast plain of unvarying dust and scrub to a huge, empty horizon.

'You're not very like your sister, are you?' he said abruptly and she turned to look at him with a resigned sigh.

'It's been said before,' she told him. 'Lucy's the pretty one. I'm the clever one,' she explained, a sardonic edge to her voice. 'Or so we've always been told.'

'Lucy doesn't strike me as stupid,' he said and Meredith laughed.

'You know, you missed your chance there to say, Oh, but you're pretty too, Meredith!'

Disconcerted by how much prettier she *did* look when she smiled, Hal returned his gaze firmly to the road ahead. 'Would you have believed me if I had?'

'Probably not,' Meredith agreed. Who was she kidding? Of *course* not. She would have despised Hal if he'd pretended that he thought she was pretty when she patently wasn't, so she was glad that he'd at least had the decency to be straight with her.

Honestly, she was glad. And it wasn't as if she cared whether he thought she was pretty or not in any case.

'That's not what I meant, anyway,' said Hal. 'I wasn't talking about looks when I said that you weren't like Lucy. I was thinking about the way Lucy loves the outback. She loves Whyman's Creek. She loves Wirrindago and the fact that we're so isolated. If she were here now, she'd be hanging out of that window with a big smile on her face.'

Meredith's heart sank. She told herself it was because her sister had clearly not yet outgrown her romantic ideals. Lucy's enthusiasms normally waned after a couple of months, but if she were still as starry-eyed about the outback as Hal suggested, Meredith might have a harder time persuading her to leave than she had anticipated.

She would rather her heart was sinking because of that than at the realisation that even the dour Hal Granger was not immune to her sister's sunny charm.

'Yes, well, Lucy's always been a romantic,' she said.

'And you're not?'

She turned away to look out of the window once more. Her eyes were hidden behind her sunglasses, but Hal guessed that they were as cool as her voice. 'No,' she said, 'I'm not.'

'Just as well,' he said. 'The outback can be a harsh place. Romantics don't tend to last very long.'

There was a distinctly dismissive note in his voice and Meredith found herself leaping to her sister's defence. 'Lucy's been here a while now,' she pointed out.

'A couple of months.' Hal brushed the idea aside with a gesture. 'I'm talking about a lifetime. In the long run, a sensible person like you would probably last longer out here than someone like Lucy with a head full of romantic ideas.'

'Frankly, I can't understand how anyone sensible would *want* to spend a lifetime here,' said Meredith, looking at the dreary landscape, the mile upon mile of nothingness unrolling towards the horizon. 'Is it all this…empty?'

Hal's gaze followed hers. 'I don't see emptiness,' he said. 'I see space. I see a big sky and no crowds. I see good grazing ground if we had a bit more rain.' He paused. 'I see home.'

'I thought you weren't a romantic?' she said with a curious glance and Hal shrugged, half embarrassed by his eloquence.

'I'm not,' he said curtly. 'I'm under no illusions about how difficult life in the bush can be.'

He was braking as he spoke and Meredith looked around in surprise. There seemed no reason to slow down on a dead straight road like this. 'Where's this?'

For answer, Hal indicated a tyre that had been cut in half and set on the corner between a dirt track and the sealed road. 'Wirrindago' had been painted around the curve of the tyre in white.

Meredith brightened and sat up straighter.

'We're here already!' she exclaimed in relief. A glance at her watch showed her that they had been driving for less than thirty minutes. 'That's much quicker than I expected. I thought you said it would take a couple of hours.'

'It will—to the homestead,' said Hal, half shaking his head at her ignorance as he swung the truck off the tarmac and on to the track.

'So this isn't your drive?' said Meredith, deflated, but reluctant to let go of her fantasy that they were almost there.

Hal thought of the track that ran across the plain, through the scrub, up into the low hills, across the creeks and paddocks and led finally to the heart of Wirrindago. He suspected Meredith's idea of a driveway was somewhat shorter.

'In a manner of speaking it is,' he told her. 'It's not a sealed road and it only goes to Wirrindago.'

That sounded promising. Meredith relaxed a little. 'Oh, well…'

'I wouldn't get your hopes up,' said Hal, seeing her imagine an early arrival. 'You might as well make yourself comfortable,' he added. 'There's a long way to go yet.'

CHAPTER TWO

THE truth of this was demonstrated barely seconds later as the truck jolted over a deep rut and Meredith found herself flung against Hal. Instinctively, she put out a hand to brace herself and realised too late that she was clutching his thigh.

'You'll have to hang on,' he told her briefly as the truck crashed into another rut.

'Hang on to what?' snapped Meredith, snatching her hand away, more ruffled than she cared to admit by the feel of his hard body, and even crosser to realise that the unexpectedly close encounter had made absolutely no impression upon Hal. He had brushed her away as if she were one of those millions and millions of annoying flies that swarmed around you the moment you stopped anywhere out here.

Flushed with a mixture of embarrassment and indignation, Meredith grabbed on to the open window and tried to brace her feet against the floor to stop herself skidding back across the seat to Hal again, but it was hard work when the truck was bouncing and lurching from side to side.

'Is it like this the whole way?'

Hal sent her a sideways glance. She looked hot and uncomfortable and her hair was sticking to her head in wind-blown clumps. Her smart outfit was covered in dust and her jaw was clenched with the effort of holding on, but she still had a certain style about her, he thought with grudging respect.

'No,' he said, 'you can't expect all the roads out here to be as good as this one, you know.'

Meredith's jaw dropped and she stared at him in appalled disbelief. *'Good?'* she echoed, her voice rising. 'This is a *good* road?'

Then she saw a faint dent at the corner of his mouth. He was obviously amused by her ignorance of the outback. Well, let him laugh. She wasn't trying to be accepted. She didn't *want* to belong here. She just wanted to find Lucy and leave him to his heat and his dust and his horrible roads as quickly as possible.

'Very funny,' she said sourly.

'It'll get better in a minute,' Hal offered by way of an apology.

'Better' was a matter of opinion, Meredith decided. The track did indeed flatten out, but instead of jolting slowly up and down the ruts, Hal put his foot down and sent the truck juddering over the corrugations at alarming speed.

'Do we have to go this fast?' she asked nervously, clinging to the window.

'It's easier at speed,' he told her. 'If you go fast enough you skip over the top of the corrugations rather than going up and down each one. Believe me, it's a lot more comfortable this way.'

'I've forgotten what comfortable means,' sighed Meredith. Her back was aching and her arms and legs were stiff from being braced at awkward angles and, as for her backside... Even its admittedly substantial padding hadn't protected it from the effects of being slammed up and down on the hard seat! She would be black and blue tomorrow.

She would never get the tangles out of her hair, she thought morosely, and that dust got *everywhere*. It was in her ears, under her nails, making her eyes gritty and insinuating itself into places she would rather not think about. The thought of sinking into a deep bath and soaking herself clean was so alluring that she found herself sighing again, until she caught Hal's eye.

'Don't tell me,' she said tartly, 'Lucy would be loving this!'

The dent in his cheek deepened. Didn't he ever smile properly? Meredith wondered irritably.

'She probably would,' he agreed, and then he slanted her another of those disconcertingly keen looks. 'What about you? What do you love? Not the bush, obviously.'

'No.' She clutched her laptop to her as she looked out of the window. There were some sparse, spindly trees breaking the monotony of the low scrub and an occasional termite mound soared out of the ground but she couldn't understand how anyone could *love* this landscape. It was all so bare. So brown. So empty.

It was just dust and glare and silence. What was there to love about that?

'No,' she said again. 'I'm a city girl. I like buildings and pavements and lights and people and noise. And I love my house,' she added, remembering it wistfully.

If only she could be there now. She could have a bath, pull the curtains in her pretty bedroom, snuggle under the duvet and sleep for a week. Bliss.

'This…' She took a hand off the dashboard to wave vaguely at the land stretching out interminably in every direction around them. 'This is just…alien.'

'What are you doing here, then?' Hal heard the harshness in his own voice and was alarmed to realise that he sounded almost disappointed.

It wasn't as if he was surprised. She had city girl written all over her, and an English city girl at that. It would be hard to find anyone who would look more out of place out here than she did.

Still, she was a stranger, and a stranger who had foisted herself upon him at that. After all that determination to get herself to Wirrindago, she could at least pretend to be interested in it.

'I told you,' she said. 'I need to see Lucy.'

'Is she expecting you? She didn't mention anything about you coming.' Hal frowned. Lucy might be a bit scatty, but he was pretty sure she would have told him if her sister was on her way.

Meredith was shaking her head, though. 'She doesn't know,' she told him. 'I've tried to get in touch with her, of course, but there's never any reply on her phone and she hasn't responded to any of the messages I've left.'

'Her phone won't work at Wirrindago,' said Hal as if it were something any fool knew. 'There's no signal out here.'

'What, none at all?'

Meredith tried to imagine life without a mobile phone, but it was like trying to imagine a thousand square kilometres. It was a different world out here, that was for sure. Her laptop felt like the only bit of normality, and she held it protectively against her side as the truck juddered over the bumpy road.

'Well, that explains why I haven't heard from Lucy for so long,' she said. 'I was getting worried.'

'Worried enough to fly all the way out to Australia?' asked Hal incredulously. 'Lucy's a little old for you to be checking up on her just because you haven't heard from her for a few weeks, isn't she?'

'I'm not checking up,' said Meredith, slightly on the defensive. 'I was just concerned in case something was wrong.'

Hal was unimpressed. 'Lucy's…what?

Twenty-four? Twenty-five? I can't believe you've come chasing to the other side of the world just because she hasn't dropped you a postcard for a couple of months!'

'It's not just that.' Meredith bit her lip. 'A friend of ours was badly injured in a car accident about ten days ago. I wanted to tell her. I tried ringing, but I didn't realise mobile phones wouldn't work out here, and when I didn't get a reply to any of my messages, of course I began to worry.'

'So you've come all this way just to give Lucy some bad news?' Hal frowned. 'Couldn't it have waited till she got home? I dare say she'll be sorry, but there's not much she can do about it out here.'

'But there is,' said Meredith. She turned her head slightly, as if looking out of the window so that he couldn't see her face. 'Richard needs her.'

Lucy. He needed Lucy, not her.

If she had expected Hal to be sympathetic, she was due for a disappointment. 'Richard's the guy who had the accident?' he said. 'Sounds to me as if he needs good medical care. Lucy's not a nurse. I don't see what she can do.'

'She can help him out of a coma.' Meredith had

hoped to be able to explain all this to Lucy first, but Hal was going to have to know why her sister was leaving. 'Richard's been unconscious ever since the accident and the doctors suggested that familiar voices might help.'

Swallowing, she stared straight ahead, one hand clutching at the window, the other the bare metal dashboard, but she wasn't seeing the outback. Instead she was in the intensive care ward, looking at Richard lying terrifyingly still in that bed, and the white, strained faces of his parents.

'Richard's parents are distraught,' she went on. 'They've been with him continually and the rest of his family have been talking to him too, but nothing seems to be working. They're convinced that Lucy's voice is the one that will help him regain consciousness.'

'It sounds to me as if they're grasping at straws,' Hal commented and Meredith turned slightly to look at him, suddenly desperate to make him understand how important it was for Lucy to go back.

'No, I'm sure they're right,' she said. 'Richard adores Lucy.' There, not even a betraying wobble in her voice, she thought, relieved. Hal wouldn't know how much it had once cost her to acknowledge that truth.

'She's the most important person in the world to him,' she went on. 'He was devastated when she left for Australia. All he wanted was for her to come back to him. If anyone can bring him back,' she assured Hal, 'Lucy can.'

'If he's going to regain consciousness he will, regardless of whether Lucy's there or not,' said Hal. 'And if he doesn't, there's not much point in her haring back to London, is there? I gather that's what you want her to do?'

Meredith nodded. 'We have to try, at least.'

'I don't see why. It sounds a lot of sentimental nonsense to me. Your Richard may "adore" Lucy, but she clearly doesn't adore him. She wouldn't have come out to Australia if she had, and I have to tell you that she hasn't been showing any signs of pining. She's been consoling herself very nicely with one of my ringers.'

Meredith wasn't entirely sure what a ringer was, but she guessed that it was probably someone who worked for Hal. She might have guessed that Lucy would have found someone else, she thought with an inward sigh. Her sister was always in love with some man or other. She had even been in love with Richard for a while, until Meredith had somehow given herself away one day.

If only she'd kept a closer guard on her expression! Richard had never guessed how she felt, and Lucy wouldn't have either if she hadn't happened to catch sight of Meredith's face in that mirror.

'Why didn't you *tell* me that you loved him?' she had demanded, stricken.

But how could she have said anything when it was obvious that Richard was head over heels in love with Lucy?

With an effort, Meredith dragged herself back to the problem in hand, all grim-featured, six-foot male of it.

'Lucy may well have found someone else, but she's still very fond of Richard,' she said. 'I'm sure she'll want to help him.'

'Maybe she will, but she's not jaunting back to London to do it,' said Hal flatly. 'She's got a job to do here.'

'You can't stop her going!' protested Meredith.

'Can't I? She's on a six-month contract, and so far she's only done two. If she wants to leave when her six months are up, that's up to her, but until then she's committed herself to staying at Wirrindago.'

Meredith stared at him in disbelief. 'But you can't mean to hold her to that when Richard's so ill! Couldn't you at least give her some compassionate leave?'

'Look, it might be different if you'd come to me and said that a member of your family was dangerously ill but, from what I can make out, this guy is just an ex-boyfriend,' said Hal callously. 'Presumably Lucy had her reasons for breaking off that relationship. I don't see why she should be expected to drop everything now and rush back to some man she's already decided she doesn't want to be with. The whole thing stinks of emotional blackmail!'

'It isn't *blackmail*!' How could he be so unfeeling? wondered Meredith furiously. If he could only *see* how ill Richard was...! But he probably wouldn't care. He obviously didn't have any feelings at all. 'I'm sure Lucy won't think that, anyway,' she told him with a defiant look that bounced right off him.

'It doesn't matter what she thinks,' he said in

an uncompromising voice. 'She's not going anywhere. The men need feeding and someone's got to look after the children. Who's going to take care of them if she goes?'

'Well, let's see…' Meredith put her head on one side and pretended to consider the matter, too cross with him to care about the fact that he was evidently married after all. Or had been. 'I know! What about *you*?' she suggested acidly.

'I've got a million acre property to run,' he said. 'I haven't got time to look after two children.'

'Perhaps you should have thought of that before you had them!'

'They're not mine,' said Hal, effectively taking the wind out of her sails. 'They're my sister's kids.'

'Oh.' Ready to be outraged at the way he was prepared to shrug aside his responsibilities as a father, Meredith was left feeling a little foolish. 'Do they live with you all the time?'

'No—thank God!' he added with feeling. 'Lydia—my sister—grew up at Wirrindago with me, but she married a city type and has been living in Sydney ever since.'

His tone made it clear what he thought about 'city types', thought Meredith, who couldn't help thinking that Lydia had probably made a good decision. If she had to choose between this god-forsaken place and the buzz of a city like Sydney, she knew which direction *she* would be heading.

'Lydia and Greg have been having some problems,' Hal went on, a tinge of distaste in his voice. 'Greg travels a lot on business, and Lydia thinks it would help if they were able to spend more time together, so she's arranged to go with him on a two month trip to Europe.'

'So you get to look after the kids while they're away?' And she thought *she'd* been asking for a big favour when she'd begged a lift to Wirrindago! Meredith reflected. Hal's sister must be a brave woman.

Hal nodded, but it was clear that the prospect of having nieces and nephews to stay left him less than enthralled. 'Lydia couldn't wait to leave Wirrindago for the city herself, but she likes the idea of an outback property, and she decided this trip was an ideal opportunity for the kids to connect with their "outback heritage", as she calls it, and for me to get to know them properly.'

The stern mouth was turned down at the corners and Meredith felt sorry for the two children sent off to stay with a grim uncle in the back of beyond. Poor kids!

'My sister and I spent a lot of time with our aunt when we were kids, so I guess she's hoping that I'll have the same kind of relationship with her children,' Hal added wryly.

'And do you?'

He lifted a shoulder. 'They've only been here a couple of days. It's obvious they don't want to be in the outback any more than I want to run a crèche but beyond that I don't really know what they're like. It's a busy time for us too, so I haven't had the chance to spend much time with them.'

'It doesn't sound very suitable,' said Meredith disapprovingly. 'Why didn't you just say *no*?'

'It's what I should have done,' Hal conceded, 'but once my sister gets an idea in her head, it's hard to shift her. She can be difficult, but she hasn't had an easy time of it and…well, I guess I just didn't know how to refuse,' he admitted in what Meredith imagined was a rare moment of weakness. 'I was the eldest, so I always had to look after her when we were growing up, and I think she's fallen into the way of relying on me.'

Meredith could sympathise with that, at least.

She had been the eldest too, and had got used to protecting Lucy.

'How old are these children?' she asked.

'Emma's nine and Mickey—Michael, I'm supposed to call him—is seven.'

Meredith frowned. 'Shouldn't they be at school?'

'They're going to do School of the Air while they're here, and Lucy's going to do some lessons with them. I made it clear in her contract that she would have to be a governess as well as a cook once the children arrived.'

'Lucy? A governess?' Meredith couldn't help laughing. *'Really?'*

Damn, there was that smile again. Hal wished she wouldn't do it. It made her look vivid and interesting and much, much harder to ignore.

'What's so funny?' he demanded gruffly.

'It just seems so unlikely,' she tried to explain. 'Governess makes me think of a Jane Eyre figure, all prim and proper, and Lucy's certainly never been that!' When you thought about Lucy, you thought about warmth and fun and laughter and a sparkling zest for life. She paused, not wanting to drop her sister in it. 'Did she tell you about her teaching experience?' she asked carefully and Hal cast her a dour smile.

'You don't need to worry; she was very open about the fact that she'd never done any. That doesn't matter to me. She doesn't have to teach them anything, just make sure that they do the work and help them with their reading and so on. It's not hard, but someone's got to be there with them. You can't leave two kids on their own all day.'

'Of course not,' said Meredith, wondering if he was expecting her to disagree.

'So you see, I can't let Lucy go now,' said Hal firmly. 'Lydia and Greg won't be back for another couple of months.'

'Couldn't—' Meredith broke off and winced as the truck went over a particularly nasty bump that shot her up in the air and then slammed her back down on to the seat. 'Couldn't you find someone else?' she tried again when she had got her breath back.

'Where?' he asked. 'It's not that easy to find people who are prepared to live on an isolated property, away from their family and friends.'

Meredith couldn't say that she was surprised.

There was no way *she* would come and live out here, no matter how fat a salary was offered.

'I was lucky to find your sister,' Hal told her. 'Lucy's got a romantic idea about what life is like in the outback, but that's fine by me. I needed a cook anyway, and once I knew Lydia was going to dump the kids on me about now, I made sure I tied her to a contract that would cover the whole time they were here. Lucy was perfectly happy to sign it,' he added.

That sounded like Lucy, thought Meredith wearily. Her sister had always been prone to wild enthusiasms, throwing herself into things with abandon before her interest waned and she was enthralled by something else entirely. It was a characteristic that exasperated Meredith even while a secret bit of her envied Lucy's ability to live for the moment.

'Lucy's never been a believer in wait and see,' she said to Hal. 'It would never occur to her to suggest a trial period before she committed herself to six months.'

'Is that what you'd have done?'

'In the unlikely event that I'd be applying for a job I'd never done before in a place I couldn't easily leave and living with people I'd never met…yes, I would certainly have insisted on a trial!'

'Then perhaps it's just as well it's Lucy who wanted the job and not you. She's certainly not regretting it, so even if she *had* been sensible like you, she would be long past the trial period by now. I think you'll find that Lucy is more than happy to stay. She's a grown woman and she can make own decisions without her big sister telling her what to do.'

Meredith flushed. She had always hated that bossy big sister image, but if even Hal Granger could see it, perhaps it was true.

But she *wasn't* bossy, she reminded herself. She wasn't always trying to tell other people what to do. She just wasn't someone who sat around waiting for things to happen. She certainly wasn't going to simply sit back and hope that Richard got better if she could make a difference by taking Lucy back to him.

'Well, let's see what Lucy has to say first,' she said, lifting her chin.

She couldn't give up now, not when she'd got this far!

Meredith stole a glance at Hal. He wasn't someone you'd want to cross if you didn't have to, she acknowledged to herself. He was toughly built and there was a competent, purposeful air about him that, as a practical person herself, she couldn't help appreciating. The trouble was that you really wanted someone like Hal on your side, rather than squaring up for a battle of wills.

Still, what could he do? He could hardly keep her and Lucy prisoners...could he? Meredith shook off the sudden doubt. Of course he couldn't. And if he *did*, they would just have to think up an escape plan.

Looking at the inhospitable terrain around her, Meredith wasn't quite sure what that would be— they certainly wouldn't be walking!—but she would just have to cross that bridge when she came to it.

Beside her, Hal saw her chin set at a stubborn angle and his eyes narrowed slightly. Meredith West seemed like someone who was used to getting her own way, and she clearly hadn't given up. If she thought she and Lucy would be able to talk him round, she was in for a disappointment, though. She had come all this way for nothing.

He felt a bit sorry for her, in fact.

'There must be other people who can talk to your Richard,' he offered. 'Why not you?'

Meredith looked at him. 'If you were longing with all your heart to see Lucy, don't you think you'd be a bit disappointed if I turned up instead?'

'But he's in a coma, you said. He won't know. He'll just be aware that there's someone there.'

'Exactly,' said Meredith. 'That's why it has to be Lucy. Richard wants to see her so much, I'm quite sure that as soon as he senses she's there, it will give him the strength to come round. If he wakes up and sees *me* sitting there, he would be so disappointed he'd probably have a relapse, and that's not what we want at all!'

She was making it into a joke, but Hal wondered about the underlying note of bleakness in her voice. He wasn't a particularly perceptive man, but it was obvious that this Richard meant a lot more to her than she was letting on.

'I'm sure you underestimate yourself,' he said.

'No, I don't.' Meredith shook her head firmly. 'Richard's not interested in me.'

She was protesting a bit too much, Hal thought. 'You seem to be going to a lot of trouble for someone who's not interested in you,' he commented mildly.

Meredith averted her face. 'He's a friend,' she said.

'Would you fly all the way out to Australia for all your friends?'

'I would if they needed me.' She turned back to him, pulling a stray strand of brown hair distastefully from her face. 'And if I could afford it. To be honest, Richard's parents paid for my ticket. They're desperate for anything that will help Richard get better, and they've pinned all their hopes on me finding Lucy.'

Hal's mouth turned down disapprovingly. 'It was a lot to ask you to do that.'

'They didn't. I offered,' said Meredith. 'I'm self-employed—I'm a freelance translator—so as long as I've got my laptop and can connect to the Internet, I can go wherever and whenever I want.' She patted the computer by her side. 'I couldn't stand sitting around waiting for news about Richard, and told them I'd rather be doing *something*. I was worried about not hearing from Lucy too, and it seemed a good opportunity to find out if she was OK.'

'So this is all your idea, in fact?'

She looked away again. 'Richard's parents kept saying how much they wished Lucy was there and it seemed like something useful I could do,' she said in a low voice. 'I would have paid for the tickets, but they insisted, and I let them pay because it made them feel that it was something *they* could do too, and obviously they can't leave Richard at the moment.'

'I see,' said Hal.

He thought he did. Meredith West was obviously one of those managing women who always thought they knew best and who decided what everyone else wanted without ever bothering to actually ask. He wouldn't be at all surprised to find that it was Meredith who had put the idea of bringing Lucy home into Richard's parents' minds.

Well, she wasn't going to manage *him*.

They drove on in silence. Meredith was so tired by this stage that her eyeballs seemed to be revolving in her head and her eyelids were so heavy that it was a huge effort to keep them from clanging down on to her lower lashes, and even that wasn't enough. Incredibly, given all the jolting and bouncing, her head kept lolling to one side until a rough lurch of the truck jerked her awake again.

To Meredith it was as if they had been driving for ever. Every now and then, they would come to a creek bed and Hal would pause, shift gears and then bump cautiously down one side and up the other. It was funny to think that sometimes these creeks would be full of water. Meredith couldn't imagine it at all. She had never been anywhere so brown and dry.

'Nearly there,' said Hal at long last, and Meredith shook herself awake and looked around her.

The landscape had changed, she realised. The dust was still that strange reddish-brown, the light still glaring, but it was rockier around here and there were sparse, spindly trees on either side of the track which made it look positively lush compared to the flat emptiness they'd been travelling through earlier.

After a while the trees thinned again and they came out on to more open land. 'That's the homestead up ahead,' said Hal, pointing into the distance.

Meredith squinted, but couldn't make out much more than a smudge of green and she was suddenly overwhelmed by the realisation of just how isolated they were, how far she was from home. This wasn't a place you could just walk away from. If Hal stuck by his refusal to allow Lucy to break her contract, how on earth would they be able to get away?

It was almost impossible to judge distances here. One minute the homestead was no more than a shimmering mirage, the next, it seemed, they were bowling past fenced paddocks and a motley collection of what seemed to Meredith to be little more than sheds with corrugated iron roofs but which Hal told her were the stockmen's quarters.

He had intended to drive through the yards and round to the side of the homestead where they could unload the stores in the back of the truck directly into the kitchen, but Meredith's expression was so unimpressed that on an impulse he changed his mind and headed round to the front of the house instead where there was a little patch of grass, lovingly irrigated to an almost startling green.

This was the best view of the old homestead, with its deep veranda and the elegant lace ironwork that was left from a less practical age, but Meredith didn't seem particularly impressed.

Why should she be? Hal wondered, annoyed with himself for even trying to give her a good impression of Wirrindago. Anyone would think he cared what she thought.

He jerked the truck to a halt at the bottom of the steps and for a moment Meredith sat numbly staring at the house in front of her, unable to believe that they had actually stopped moving.

It was a much bigger building than she had imagined, somehow. Bigger and older and more substantial in spite of the iron roof. The walls, almost hidden in the shadows of the veranda, were of solid stone and the door and windows hinted at a faded grandeur. This had once been a gracious home, she realised in surprise, but times had evidently been less gracious for a long time now. There were distinct signs of neglect— or perhaps of an ungracious owner, she thought, sliding a sidelong glance at Hal.

He seemed to be in a bad mood again. Getting out of the truck, he slammed the door as he spotted two sulky-looking children on the veranda. The girl was slumped in the chair, while the little boy's head was bent intently over a computer game.

'Uncle Hal's back,' Meredith heard one of them shout inside the house, but neither of them made any move to come down and greet them.

Bad move, thought Meredith as she saw Hal's brows snap together in that forbidding frown.

'You two can come and help take all this stuff to the kitchen,' he snapped, moving round to the back of the truck.

'Oh…do we *have* to?' moaned the girl.

'Yes, you do. You too, Mickey.'

'I'm just finishing this game—'

'*Now!*'

Evidently Hal didn't believe in reasoning with children. No wonder the children looked sulky, thought Meredith. It worked, though. Mickey put down his computer game and trailed down the steps after his equally reluctant sister, but both stopped dead and stared when Meredith got stiffly out of the truck and stretched.

Hal followed the children's glances. She looked decidedly the worse for wear. Her suit was rumpled, her hair a wild bush around her head and she was swaying with tiredness, but he had to admit that there was a certain style about her. Putting a hand to the small of her back, she stretched and winced at the soreness of her muscles.

'Emma and Mickey, you'd better come and say hello to—' he began, only to find himself interrupted by Lucy, who had come out of the door and was standing at the top of the steps, staring in disbelief at her sister.

'*Meredith?*' she said, astounded.

'Hi, Lucy.' Thousands of miles she had travelled, and that was all she could say!

Shaken out of her trance, Lucy came hurrying down the steps to sweep Meredith into a warm hug.

'I can't believe it's really you!' she cried. 'It's so good to see you.' Then she pulled back to hold Meredith at arm's length as her beautiful blue eyes darkened with puzzlement. 'But what on *earth* are you doing here?'

CHAPTER THREE

'POOR Richard!' said Lucy again, shaking her blonde head as she tried to take in Meredith's news. 'I can't believe it. And his poor parents! They must be worried sick.'

'They are.'

Meredith was sitting at the kitchen table, drinking a mug of tea and explaining what had happened. There had only been time to give Lucy the bare bones when she'd arrived. Hal, for all his grumpiness, had insisted that she have a shower and a sleep before she did anything else, and Meredith had to admit that she was feeling a lot better for it.

Now she watched her sister preparing the supper and tried to think how best to raise the question of going home. Hal had warned her that Lucy was enjoying outback life and, much as Meredith had wanted to believe that he was wrong, it was obvious that her sister was very happy. She was going to have to lead up to the real reason she was here very gradually.

Lucy was a good cook, but a notoriously messy one, and Meredith had to fight all her instincts to get up and start tidying up after her. But she knew it would annoy Lucy if she did, so she averted her eyes from the mess and sat, turning the mug of tea between her hands and wondering how to start.

'Poor you, too.' Lucy turned up the heat under a pan of potatoes and turned to lean back against the worktop, her blue eyes serious for once as she regarded her elder sister.

'Me?' Meredith looked up from her tea in surprise.

'I know how you feel about Richard,' said Lucy gently. 'It must be awful for you too.'

'I'm all right,' said Meredith in a brisk voice, hoping to ward off any further questions, but Lucy patently wasn't convinced.

'Meredith, I'm your sister,' she said. 'You don't have to pretend to be Superwoman with me.'

'That pan's boiling over,' said Meredith, nodding to the stove beside Lucy.

Lucy turned obediently to lift the lid and reduce the heat under the pan, but she cast a beady glance over her shoulder at Meredith as she did so. 'Don't change the subject!'

'I'm not. I haven't the faintest idea what you're talking about. I've never thought of myself as Superwoman!'

'You might not think you are, but you've never been prepared to admit that you might be lonely or scared or unhappy like the rest of us,' said Lucy, adding salt to the pan. 'I know you're in love with Richard. What's wrong with admitting that you're heartbroken and sick with worry about him?'

Unable to sit still any longer, Meredith got up and began clearing the dishes out of the sink where Lucy had dumped them as she'd gone along.

'You always romanticise everything, Lucy,' she said crossly. 'I'm not *heartbroken*. Yes, there was a time when I hoped that Richard and I would get together… but it didn't work out. He fell in love with you instead,' she said, her voice carefully neutral. 'I don't blame him for that, and I certainly don't blame you.'

'Maybe you should blame yourself,' Lucy suggested, and Meredith turned in surprise at the unexpected note of exasperation in Lucy's voice, a bowl still in her hands.

'Did it ever occur to you that if you had given Richard the slightest encouragement, he probably wouldn't have fallen for me?' Lucy went on.

Meredith rolled her eyes. 'Right, a man like Richard is going to think, Hmm, here's someone plain and dumpy, but over *there* is a tall, slim beauty…I know! I'll go for the short, fat one!'

'He might have done if you'd ever let him close enough to find out what you're really like,' said Lucy. 'And you are *not* plain! You've got beautiful skin and your eyes are gorgeous, and I know loads of women who'd give their eye teeth for your cleavage.

'You should try showing off your body some time, not hiding it away,' she scolded Meredith, who had turned back to the sink, having heard this argument many times before. 'Richard probably didn't know that you *had* a cleavage! You were so busy being careful and not letting him guess how you felt that he thought you were only interested in being good friends, and of course then he's going to start looking around.

'I just happened to be the first likely person he came across,' she said, 'and if you had told *me*, I would never have thought about going out with him, and we could have saved ourselves the whole mess!'

Lucy stared in exasperation at her sister's unresponsive back, but something about the set of those shoulders made her relent suddenly. With a sigh, she went over and hugged Meredith.

'I'm sorry,' she said guiltily. 'I'm *sorry*. The last thing you need after that journey is me having a go at you. I just want you to be happy, as happy as I am now with Kevin, and you won't be as long as you keep everything bottled up like this.'

Meredith could feel tears pricking behind her eyes and she blinked them away furiously. She must be even more tired than she had thought.

Setting the last of the pans on the work surface, she wiped out the sink and began to run the hot water. 'I'm not bottling things up, Lucy, I promise you,' she said. 'I was—I *am*—fine about you and Richard. There was no need for you to throw everything up and dash off to Australia.'

'I felt so *awful* when I realised how you felt about him,' Lucy tried to explain. 'But it wasn't just that, to be honest. I was bored with my job and…well, Richard's lovely, but we didn't go out for very long, and it was never that serious.'

'It was for him.' Meredith turned off the tap and turned to face Lucy. 'He really loves you.'

'You can't know that.'

'I do.'

Meredith wasn't going to tell Lucy about the evenings Richard had spent with her, talking about how much he loved Lucy, how empty life was without her, wondering what he had done to make her leave so suddenly. Meredith had listened and comforted him as best she could. It had seemed all that she could do for him, but she had never told him the real reason Lucy had left. She had told herself that Lucy would soon get bored with Australia, that she would come home and Richard would have another chance to be happy.

But she had left it too late.

Lucy was bending to take a huge joint of beef out of the oven. 'Richard didn't seem that upset when I left,' she said.

'He didn't want to make things difficult for you,' said Meredith. 'Lucy, you're really impor-tant to Richard. He needs you now.'

Biting her lip, Lucy basted the joint. 'I wish there was something I could do to help.'

'There is.' Meredith took a breath. 'I think— it's not just me, though, his parents and the doctors think it too—we *all* think that the sound of your voice might be what it takes to bring Richard round.'

Lucy's head came up at that, and she froze in mid-baste. *'What?'*

'The doctors told us to keep talking to him,' Meredith hurried on, 'so that's what everyone's been doing, but I'm sure it's you he wants to hear. I'm sure he would wake up for you.'

To her horror, she found her voice cracking a little at the end and she clamped her lips together in a fiercely straight line for a moment. 'I just think that if you were to sit next to him,' she went on after drawing a steadying breath, 'if you were to hold his hand and tell him that you were there, I think Richard would make that extra effort that he needs.'

Lucy put the roast back in the oven. 'You want me to go back to London?' she said in a dull voice.

'Yes.' Meredith nodded eagerly. 'Richard's parents have given me the money for your ticket. They just want you there as soon as possible.' She paused, seeing the reluctance in her sister's expression. 'It wouldn't be for ever, Lucy. You could come back to Australia as soon as Richard was out of danger, but…yes, please come back with me,' she said. 'It would mean so much to Richard.'

'And to you?' asked Lucy.

Meredith looked away, unable to meet her eyes. 'I just want him to get better,' she said in a low voice. 'That's all.'

Lucy sighed. Pulling out a chair, she sat down at the table and rubbed her eyes. 'I'm on a contract,' she said. 'I'm committed to staying here for another four months, at least.'

'Hal Granger told me about that,' said Meredith. 'It sounds to me as if he was taking advantage of you, Lucy. He can't hold you to it if you want to leave.'

'But that's just it, I *don't* want to leave,' Lucy confessed, raising her head. 'I love it here.'

She half smiled at Meredith's expression. 'I know it's not your kind of place, but I feel as if I've finally found the place I want to be and the man I want to be with.'

'You've fallen in love again?' said Meredith, resigned, and Lucy bridled.

'Don't say it like that! This time it's for real…it *is*!' she insisted, offended by her sister's sceptical expression. 'Kevin's different from anyone else I've ever met. You'll understand when you meet him.

'He's so…' She hugged her arms together, trying to find the words to describe him. 'Well, he's special,' was the best she could come up with. 'It's an incredible feeling when you look at someone and your knees go week, and you just think, *That's the one*!'

Meredith didn't say anything. She was thinking about the first time she had met Richard. She had taken one look into his smiling brown eyes and her heart had done a strange flip. *There you are*, she had thought. *I've been waiting my whole life for you.*

'I really *love* him,' Lucy was saying, 'and I'm sure—well, almost sure—that Kevin feels the same way about me. We've been getting on really well. Kevin's not someone who rushes into things—he's not like me, which is a good thing, isn't it?—but I've just got this feeling, *here*,' she said, thumping her heart, 'that's it's meant to be.'

'I see,' said Meredith flatly.

'It's not that I don't want to help Richard,' Lucy said. 'I do. I'm very fond of him. He'll always be a friend and, even if he wasn't, I'd do it for you, Meredith, but…'

She bit her lip. 'If I go, I won't be able to come back,' she said. 'Hal Granger is a hard man. He'd be furious with me if I broke my contract, and I know he wouldn't let me come back. And how could I leave Emma and Mickey on their own? The poor kids have just arrived and they're horribly homesick. Hal's too busy to look after them and—'

Lucy stopped abruptly, catching sight of the look on Meredith's face. She covered her face with her hands and shook her head slowly. 'Listen to me,' she said, appalled at herself. 'I shouldn't be talking like this when Richard's so ill. I'm sorry, Meredith.'

Lowering her hands, she took a deep breath. 'Do you really think it will make such a difference if I go back?'

It was Meredith's turn to hesitate. She hadn't realised until now quite what she was asking Lucy to give up. 'Yes, I do,' she said slowly. 'I wish we had some way of finding out how he was. If he's come round already, then of course there would be no need for you to go back, but how can we know? I tried ringing Richard's mother when I got here, but then I remembered that my phone wouldn't work.'

'I'll ask Hal if we can use the phone in the office,' said Lucy, pushing back her chair. 'He's hard, but he's not mean.'

Barely five minutes later, Meredith was listening to Richard's mother weeping down the phone. 'He's still just *lying* there,' she said through her tears. 'We're at our wits' end. The doctors say we need to find something to stimulate him, but we've tried *everything*. If only Lucy were here! Have you found out where she is yet?'

Meredith hesitated, not wanting to commit her sister to anything before she was ready, but Lucy, who had been listening in, reached calmly across and took the phone from her.

'Yes, she's found me, Ellen. I'm coming back as soon as I can.'

'Lucy…' said Meredith a little helplessly when she had put down the phone.

'It's OK.' Lucy smiled at her. 'Richard being ill didn't seem quite real when you told me about it, but hearing Ellen so upset brought it home to me. Of course I'll go back.'

'What about Kevin?'

'He'll wait for me,' said Lucy, determinedly bright. 'I know he will. I'll come back to him. Something will turn up. Maybe he could find a job on another station and I could join him there.'

'Or,' said Meredith slowly, 'you could come back here.'

Lucy shook her head. 'I wish I could, but Hal is a man who means what he says. If I break my contract now, there's no way I'd ever be able to come back. Don't worry about it, Meredith. It's Richard that matters, really, and there's nothing you can do about Hal.'

But Meredith wasn't a girl who liked to be told that there was nothing she could do. Her lips pressed together in a determined way and there was a look in her eye as she thought through her plan that Lucy recognised with a little lift of her heart. When Meredith looked like that, Meredith made things happen.

'We'll see about that,' she said.

* * *

The homestead was much bigger and more rambling than it seemed from outside, and it took Meredith some time to find Hal. Preoccupied by supper and the decision she had just made, Lucy had waved vaguely in the direction of the back of the house and said he would probably be on the back veranda.

He was. At least, Meredith assumed that it was the back veranda, since that was where she found him. He had showered and shaved and was wearing clean jeans and a faded red shirt, although she didn't notice at first.

'Oh,' she said as the screen door that separated every room from the outside clattered to behind her and she found herself staring at quite the most spectacular sunset she had ever seen.

The kitchen was on the other side of the house and, although she had been vaguely aware that the light was fading, nothing had prepared her to step through the door into a blaze of gold and red and orange. It was so dramatic that for a long moment she could just stand and gape.

'It's quite something, isn't it?' Hal's voice from the end of the veranda startled her out of her trance and she walked slowly down to join him, her eyes still on the sunset.

'It's beautiful,' she acknowledged. 'But a bit overwhelming too. It's so big and so...so *there*. You feel like you could almost reach out and touch it.'

'Watch,' said Hal, and she stood next to him in silence as the golden sky flushed deeper and deeper until it was a fiery red and the range of bare hills in the distance darkened into purple and then black. A strange hush marked the moment when the great ball of the sun sank behind below the horizon, and the breath caught at the back of Meredith's throat. It was as if the earth itself had stopped turning and the whole world was waiting for a sign that the evening could begin.

And then, quite suddenly, it was over. An insect rasped somewhere. She could hear Lucy clattering dishes in the kitchen and Emma and Mickey's voices raised in a squabble.

Meredith let out a shaky breath and cleared her throat. 'Gosh,' she said weakly.

Hal was glad that the sunset at least had impressed her. Nothing else about the outback had.

Then he wondered why he cared whether she was impressed or not.

And why he was so aware of her standing next to him.

'You're looking better,' he said gruffly.

Meredith put a hand up to her clean hair, remembering with a grimace how long it had taken her to wash out the dust and the tangles. 'I certainly feel better,' she said. 'I don't know how long it will take to get all the sand out of the shower, though. I've never been that gritty before!'

She didn't look gritty now. She looked soft and warm and voluptuous, and Hal could actually feel his hand tingling with the temptation to reach out and see if her skin felt as smooth as it looked.

Averting his eyes, he leant on the veranda rail and wished she hadn't mentioned being in the shower, wished he wasn't finding it quite so easy to picture her there. In spite of keeping his gaze fixed firmly on the darkening sky ahead, he was very conscious of her body as she stood beside him, which was strange as she was doing absolutely nothing to draw attention to it.

The loose, flowing skirt and top with its

V-neck and three-quarter-length sleeves could hardly have been less revealing. The skirt was a little out of place, but otherwise Hal had to admit that she was dressed sensibly enough, certainly more so than she had been earlier.

So there was no reason to notice that the top outlined curves that he hadn't noticed before. No reason to find her feminine and somehow alluring, in spite of the fact that her expression was perfectly composed. She was cool and businesslike and not in the least interested in trying to attract him.

Any more than he wanted to be attracted.

'I was wondering if I could have a word,' she said, sounding exactly as if she had popped her head round an office door to talk to a colleague.

The realisation that she was all business while he was struggling like an awkward adolescent to keep his eyes off her riled Hal.

'If you're going to try and talk me into changing my mind about Lucy, forget it,' he said brusquely. 'I made the situation clear when I hired her and she accepted the conditions.'

'I appreciate that,' said Meredith, 'but I do have a proposal to put to you.'

Hal scowled. Why did she have to make everything sound like a business strategy? Why couldn't she sound sultry and seductive, the way that mouth should sound? 'What sort of proposal?' he asked suspiciously.

'A sensible one, I think.'

It would be, of course. She might have a body meant for fun and flirtation, but Hal was prepared to bet that Meredith's head would always stay cool and clear.

'As far as I'm concerned, the only sensible solution is for Lucy to stay and do the job she's contracted to do,' he said.

'But it's getting the job done that's important to you, rather than who does it?'

'I guess so,' he said grudgingly, wondering where all this was going.

'Then it wouldn't matter to you if I took Lucy's place and did the job for her, would it?'

'You?' Hal straightened from the rail in surprise. He wasn't quite sure what he had been expecting her to say, but it certainly hadn't been that.

'Why not?' said Meredith coolly. 'I'm quite capable. I can do everything Lucy can do. I can cook and, while I don't have much experience of children either, I don't see why I shouldn't help Emma and Mickey with their lessons. I've got a degree and they're not going to be studying brain surgery, are they?'

She looked, thought Hal, completely serious, and for a moment he could only stare at her, trying to think of a reason why it was so obviously a ridiculous idea. 'You would hate it out here,' he said at last and Meredith shrugged.

'I'm not proposing to stay long,' she pointed out. 'Just long enough for Lucy to get to England, do what she can for Richard and come back as soon as possible.'

'And how long will that be?'

'That depends how Richard is. We can't tell until she gets to the hospital. Maybe two or three weeks?'

Two or three weeks with Meredith. The thought was unaccountably unsettling and Hal frowned.

'You're determined for her to go, aren't you?' he said. 'Do you always get your own way?'

'If I had my way, I would be leaving with Lucy,' said Meredith tartly. 'The fact that I'm offering to stay here is entirely due to the fact that *you* are determined to have *your* way.'

She met Hal's gaze, her own bright with challenge. 'Lucy loves it here,' she told him. 'More than anything else, she wants to be able to come back, but you've made it clear that she can't do that if she chooses to help Richard. I know she's only agreed to that for my sake, so the least I can do is to keep her job open for her. I don't see what difference it makes to you, anyway,' she finished. 'I'll do everything Lucy does.'

Hal couldn't really think what difference it would make either. He just knew that it would. Lucy fitted easily into the homestead. She was friendly and relaxed and everything was the same when she was around.

Meredith was different. She would change things, Hal knew she would. She was changing things just by standing there. There was something challenging about her, something that made him feel edgy and slightly defensive, and Hal didn't like it.

'What about your job?' he prevaricated. 'Can you take three weeks off just like that?'

'You've got a phone line, haven't you?'

'Yes,' he admitted.

'Well, then.' Meredith seemed to think that

solved the problem. 'I'm freelance, as I told you,' she said. 'If I can connect to the Internet, I can work. I've got all my files on my laptop and I can contact clients by email. They won't know that I'm in Australia. It's not ideal, but it's perfectly possible for me to carry on as normal.'

'Except that you're not going to have time for working if you're planning to do everything Lucy does,' Hal pointed out. 'You're going to have to provide proper meals for seven men and two children every day, and often there'll be other people around as well. You could be cooking for twelve or fifteen or even twenty people sometimes. They'll all need breakfast, lunch and supper, and then there's smoko twice a day.'

'Smoko?' Meredith echoed dubiously, her heart sinking at the thought of all those meals. She was used to cooking for one, not ten!

'It gets hot out there,' said Hal. 'The men start early and traditionally they stop for a cup of tea and smoke halfway through the morning, and then again in the afternoon. They like a bit of cake or biscuit or something then too. Personally, I'm very fond of a rock cake.'

Rock cakes. Fine. Meredith gritted her teeth on a sigh. 'I expect I can manage those.'

'And then there's all the cleaning,' Hal went on, rather enjoying her growing dismay as he pointed out exactly what she had so confidently offered to take on. 'Lucy's housekeeper as well as cook, so she cleans the homestead, does the laundry, monitors the radio and keeps an eye on the garden.'

Meredith did sigh this time. 'What did your last slave die of?' she asked, and Hal gave a grim smile.

'I haven't finished,' he said. 'Now she has to look after the kids too. They'll be starting School of the Air on Monday. That means they'll have to be at the radio at the set times, and then they'll have to do correspondence work for five or six hours, all of which has to be supervised. Most outback kids are used to working like that, but Emma and Mickey are from Sydney and they're going to need more help getting their lessons done.'

'Are you trying to put me off?' asked Meredith sweetly. 'Because, believe me, there's no need. I was put off quite enough before you started!'

'I'm just trying to point out that you won't have a lot of time for your own work.'

She lifted her chin. 'I'll find time.'

'That's up to you,' said Hal, 'but don't think you can get away with skimping on the job in order to catch up on your own work. I'll agree to let Lucy go, but only if you're prepared to do the job properly.'

'I always do a proper job,' said Meredith coldly.

Looking at her, Hal could believe it. She was off-puttingly competent, with a body that couldn't have been more *un*businesslike.

The body that he was not supposed to be noticing at all. He turned to lean back against the railings and cross his arms, thereby keeping his hands firmly under control.

'What about the rest of your life?'

It was Meredith's turn to look puzzled. 'What do you mean?'

'Lucy might be away for a few weeks—as you say, it'll depend on if and when your Richard comes round—so you could be stuck out here for a while. Not many people can just walk away from their lives without warning the way you're proposing to do.'

'I told you, I'm self-employed,' she said. 'If I work, which I will, I'll be earning. My mortgage and bills are paid on direct debit. I've got no pets, not even a cat, and the alarm is on at my house. The post may build up a bit, but otherwise I think everything should be under control.'

Of course. Meredith's life was probably always under control.

'What about boyfriends?'

'What about them?' she asked stiffly.

'I wouldn't be that pleased if my girlfriend told me that she was going away for a short trip and ended up staying away for weeks.'

Especially not if his girlfriend had a body like hers and he was used to losing himself in her softness and her warmth.

Hal refolded his arms more firmly.

'There isn't anybody special at the moment,' said Meredith after a tiny pause. 'Not that it's any of your business,' she added.

'It is if you start getting yearning phone calls, begging you to come home,' Hal pointed out. 'It is if you end up distracted and having to choose between your sister and your boyfriend. That wouldn't be an easy choice to make.'

'Yes, well, I don't think you need to worry,' said Meredith, with just the slightest trace of bitterness.

'I'm not exactly overwhelmed with yearning lovers, and even if I were, I wouldn't find it at all difficult to make my choice. I've said that I'll stay here and take Lucy's place, and I will.'

'I don't know…' Hal regarded her with a brooding expression. 'It's easy to say that, but what happens when you're struggling to get everything done and you hate the heat and the flies and you're bored and lonely? There'll be nothing to stop you changing your mind and running back to England the moment the going gets tough.'

'Nothing except my word,' said Meredith, lifting her chin at him. 'I'm not expecting to like it here. I'm quite sure I *will* be bored and I hate the heat and flies already, but none of that matters. I've promised Lucy that I'll stay as long as necessary so that she can come back to her job, and I always keep my promises.'

'I've heard that before.' Hal's voice was hard. 'As far as I can see, the promises women make don't seem to mean much.'

'Then you're just going to have to trust me, aren't you?' said Meredith, wondering who had made him that bitter. 'You might as well. If you don't, you won't have a cook at all. I know Lucy.

She's someone else who always keeps her promises, and she's promised Richard's mother that she'll go back to see if she can help. She won't stay now, so if you're sensible you'll take me in her place,' she went on crisply. 'At least then you'll have someone to help, as opposed to no one at all.'

Hal eyed her with frustration. He knew that she was right, but he couldn't help resenting the way she appeared to be rearranging his life to suit herself. 'Are you always like this?' he demanded, scowling.

'Like what?'

'This…managing,' he said, having searched for the right word. 'I don't like being managed,' he warned her. 'I've been running this property for nearly fifteen years. If there's any managing to be done, I'm the one that likes to do it!'

'I'm not *managing* you,' Meredith objected. 'I'm just offering a practical solution to the problem.'

'There wasn't any problem until you came along,' he grumbled.

'Well, there is now,' she said in a brisk voice, 'so, one way or another, you're going to have to deal with it.'

'Oh, very well,' he conceded irritably. 'If you're so determined to stay, stay!'

'Thank you,' said Meredith, cool as ever. 'There is just one thing more, though.'

Hal muttered under his breath, 'What *now*?'

'I want you to promise that Lucy can have her job back whenever she wants.'

'You're pushing it a bit, aren't you?' he said, his eyes narrowed. 'I don't think you're in a position to demand promises from me.'

'That's the deal,' she said stubbornly. 'I'll only stay if you'll promise to keep Lucy's job for her.'

With an irritable gesture, Hal pushed himself away from the rail. 'Fine, I'm prepared to promise that, but you're not leaving a second before she gets back. If you leave, the deal's off.'

'Good,' said Meredith. 'We've got a deal.'

'Deal.'

Without thinking, Hal held out his hand and, after a moment's hesitation, she took it. His fingers closing around hers, warm and strong, sent a strange sensation down Meredith's spine. It was too dark to read the expression in his eyes properly, but something in his face as she looked up at him made her pull her hand away rather too quickly and she was suddenly, unaccountably, breathless.

'Deal,' she said.

CHAPTER FOUR

MEREDITH was so tired by the time they sat down to the meal that night that it was all she could do to lift her knife and fork. She had been travelling for days, and had been so worried about Richard before she'd left that she had barely slept all week. But now she had found her sister, Lucy was going home, and that meant that at last Meredith could simply stop for a while.

Stop she did, literally flaking out over her roast beef and vegetables, and the next morning barely remembered Lucy helping her to bed. She was left with no more than a blurry impression of taciturn stockmen and sulky children. Hal was looking dour, and the only sunny natures there appeared to be Lucy, glowing happily up at a quiet young man—Kevin, Meredith assumed—and Hal's cousin, Guy Dangerfield.

Guy, to Meredith's surprise, proved to be as

English as she was, defying the national stereotype even more than his cousin. Where Hal was dark and reserved and buttoned-up, Guy oozed a kind of lazy, good-humoured charm that even Meredith, normally charm-proof, found impossible to resist. It wasn't just that Guy was attractive, with dark blond hair and dancing blue eyes, he was *funny*, not so much in what he said but in the way that he said it. His dry delivery even made Hal laugh, and *that* was quite something to see.

The first time it happened, Meredith was caught unawares. She was helping Lucy to carry in the vegetables and was just setting a dish of carrots on the table when Guy said something that made Hal throw back his head with a crack of laughter. The transformation of his face was so extraordinary that Meredith actually dropped the dish.

Fortunately, it didn't have far to fall and only a few carrots spilled out, but of course they all stopped to look at her.

'Sorry,' she muttered, hastily scooping up carrots. 'It was just a bit hot.'

Please God none of them would think to reach out and touch the dish or they'd discover it was barely warm. Lucy had never got the hang of warming plates. She would just have to plead jet lag if that happened, Meredith decided, pink with embarrassment. There was no way she was going to admit how startled she had been by the way Hal's whole expression had lightened with a smile, the way the cool grey eyes had warmed and the cheeks had creased with amusement. His teeth had been strong and white, and he had looked at once much younger and much, much more attractive.

Perhaps it was a good thing that he didn't smile more often, Meredith reflected. It was just as well that Guy was leaving tomorrow and taking his humour with him.

Guy, in fact, had solved the final problem about getting Lucy home. 'Your timing couldn't be better,' he told Meredith. 'I spend a couple of weeks here every year and I've been putting off going home as long as possible, but I really do have to go now. My mother, who is not the easiest person at the best of times, is having her hip replaced, so I need to be there.'

He rolled his eyes with a rueful smile, but Meredith guessed that he was very fond of his mother, difficult or not. 'I'll probably just annoy her but, if I know my mother, she'll be even more annoyed if I'm not there.'

A plane had been chartered to take him to Darwin the next morning and the pilot would be picking him up at the Wirrindago airstrip, Guy explained. It would make perfect sense if Lucy went with him. They could travel together and save Hal another trip into Whyman's Creek, and Lucy might as well catch the same plane to London. He would even have a car meeting him at Heathrow so she could go all the way to central London without having to worry about a thing.

It sounded a great plan to Meredith and Hal had no objection. The only person who wasn't happy was Lucy herself, although she could hardly insist on Hal making another trip to Whyman's Creek so that she could travel separately from Guy.

Oddly, she alone seemed to be immune to Guy's charm. 'He's just a trust fund baby,' she said dismissively when she and Meredith were on their own in the kitchen. 'He's not a real man like Kevin.'

Real man or not, it seemed to Meredith that Guy was brighter, better-looking and a lot more fun than Kevin. There was no accounting for taste. Personally, she approved of Guy, who was a lot more practical than one would guess from a first impression. It was Guy who got things organised and who sorted the flights while Lucy was saying an emotional farewell to Kevin.

Meredith woke late that morning with the sick feeling that she had left something vitally important undone. Scrambling out of bed, she rushed along to try and book Lucy on to the London flight from Darwin and was pleasantly surprised to discover that Guy had already done it all. For someone used to dealing with everything herself, it was a huge treat to find that she could relax for once.

Now she stood on the dusty airstrip next to Hal and waved as the little plane that Guy had chartered sped down the runway. Looking like a toy, it lifted up into a sky so blue and so enormous that it made Meredith's eyes ache behind her sunglasses.

Beside her, Hal wore a hat, his eyes narrowed against the glare as he watched the plane disappear into the blueness. The red dust churned up by the take-off was drifting back to earth and the silence once they had gone seemed to settle around them like an immense weight.

The sheer size of the horizon and the stillness of the landscape was overwhelming. Meredith felt tiny in comparison and she thought that if Hal hadn't been standing beside her she would have been almost frightened by the uncanny sensation that the land was waiting for something.

As it was, Hal's solid, self-contained presence was immensely reassuring. Outlined against the dusty backdrop of spindly gum-trees and scrub, his profile was extraordinarily distinct in the crystalline light. Meredith was sure that she could see every pore in his skin, every quirk in the battered felt hat. He wore a pair of faded jeans and scuffed boots, his sleeves were rolled up above his wrists, and his hands were brown and steady. He looked completely at home in this strange, alien place and Meredith was suddenly conscious of a childish urge to hold on to him and feel safe.

'We'd better get on,' he said.

'Yes,' said Meredith briskly. Enough of this. She was a sensible woman. Of course she didn't need Hal to feel safe. Whatever next? This was Australia, not the end of the world.

It just felt like it.

She put her shoulders back as Hal turned to the truck parked in the meagre shade. Beside it, Meredith had been chagrined to notice earlier, stood a small plane with a propeller on its nose.

'Why didn't you fly into Whyman's Creek yesterday?' she had asked when Hal admitted that it was his. 'It would have been a lot more comfortable than two hours in that truck!'

'I want Jed to have a look at the tail rudder,' Hal said. 'He's the mechanic, but he hasn't got time at the moment. He's been checking the water pumps, which is more important than being comfortable on a trip into town.'

That, thought, Meredith, was a matter of opinion.

The plane looked awfully small, she decided, eyeing it askance as she followed Hal to the truck. Under normal circumstances, she wouldn't have set foot in it, but she couldn't help hoping that Jed got round to fixing it before Lucy came back. A flight would be much more comfortable, and a lot less dirty, than another bone-shaking trip into Whyman's Creek before she caught the plane home.

Home...Meredith looked around her at the

eerily silent scrub and sighed. Her cosy house in Tooting seemed very far away.

'You can get in the cab this time,' Hal pointed out as he opened his door.

'Big of you,' muttered Meredith. The airstrip was about half a mile from the homestead and there hadn't been room for more than three in the front seat. Meredith had wanted to say goodbye to Lucy at the plane, and as Hal had to drive and Guy and Lucy had a long trip ahead of them, it had made sense that she'd been the one who had sat in the back with the suitcases. By the time they had jolted down to the end of the track, she had been wishing that she'd said goodbye at the homestead as Hal had suggested.

He must have known that she would end up covered in dust—again!

'I'm not sure that sitting inside is going to make much difference to this outfit now,' she said, grimacing down at her pale trousers and sleeveless white top. Well, it had been white when she had put it on that morning.

'Haven't you got anything more practical to wear?' Hal asked as she climbed into the cab anyway.

'No,' said Meredith, who thought she had done well to find these trousers.

He switched on the engine and the truck juddered into life. 'I'd have thought you could have packed something a bit more sensible,' he said disapprovingly.

'My wardrobe is perfectly sensible for what I thought I'd be doing,' Meredith objected. 'I didn't realise I would be put in the back of an open truck and driven through a dust bowl! So far I've ruined two outfits,' she remembered glumly. 'At this rate, I won't have anything to wear at all next week! I'll be cooking in my underwear.'

Hal raised his eyebrows. 'That sounds interesting,' he said.

His voice was dry but when he glanced at her Meredith realised with a tiny shock of recognition that the cool eyes held a distinct gleam of amusement and a shiver of something that was perilously close to excitement skittered down her spine.

More worryingly, her palm was actually tingling with the memory of how it had felt to touch his hand last night. 'Deal,' they had said, and his fingers had closed around hers. She shouldn't be able to remember *exactly* how that had felt, Meredith chided herself. She shouldn't be wondering what it would be like to feel the warmth and sureness of his hands on her again.

Her mouth dried at the very idea, but luckily Hal was changing the subject without waiting for her to think of a suitably pithy answer.

'Did Lucy have time to show you round?' he asked, sounding so prosaic that Meredith wondered if she had imagined the awareness that had sparked in that brief glance a moment ago.

Embarrassed by what felt like a betraying flush in her cheeks, she clutched the dashboard and looked out of the window. 'No. She was busy cooking the meal last night and I'm afraid it was all a bit of a rush this morning. She had her own stuff to pack, and I'd slept late.'

'You were tired.'

'Yes, I'm sorry about last night,' said Meredith a little stiffly. 'One minute I was eating beef and the next my head was in the gravy. I was completely zonked.'

'Are you going to be OK to do lunch today?'

'Of course,' she said quickly, reading criticism in his tone. 'I said I could do Lucy's job, and I will.'

Hal glanced at her. 'I'd better show you where everything is, in that case. It'll save you a bit of time.'

Emma and Mickey were still in bed, in spite of strict instructions to be up and dressed by the time Hal and Meredith got back from the airstrip. Hal hauled them up and sent them grumbling along to the kitchen to find their own breakfast while he gave Meredith a brisk tour of the homestead.

Some of it she remembered from the night before. There was the austere dining area that opened out from the kitchen. A long, rectangular table sat on the painted concrete floor, dominating the room, but for Meredith the most noticeable feature was the way an entire wall had been left open to the air, but screened off to keep the insects out.

Another screened veranda led from the other side of the kitchen. It was more comfortable-looking, with a number of old wicker chairs ranged in a rough semicircle facing the screen. Lucy had told her that they all gathered there for a cold beer before supper but, having watched her sister at work, Meredith couldn't imagine ever having the time to sit down herself.

Hal pointed out the store rooms, the laundry room and a whole wall of stainless steel fridges and freezers of varying temperatures.

'And this is the cold store,' he said, opening a door.

'Ugh!' Meredith recoiled at the sight of the carcass hanging from a butcher's hook. 'What's that?'

'It was a cow and now it's food,' said Hal.

'I hope you're not expecting *me* to chop it up!'

'No.' Hal gritted his teeth and hung on to his patience. 'One of the men will butcher it for you when you need more meat. There's still a couple of joints left,' he went on, indicating some smaller cuts hanging at the side. 'Those are for roasting or steaks. There's a mincing machine as well, if you want it, and I think Lucy should have some diced meat for stewing in the freezer.'

Meredith grimaced. She was used to her meat wrapped in nice sanitised packets at the supermarket, where you never had to think about where it had come from or what it had once been.

'What happens when that one's finished?' she asked, averting her eyes from the carcass.

Hal looked at her. 'What do you think?'

Meredith's mouth turned down even further. She didn't like to think of some poor cow being slaughtered on her say-so. 'What do you give vegetarians?'

'We don't get a lot of those on a cattle station,' he said, closing the door. 'We eat beef. Beef, beef and more beef.'

'I do a very nice spinach quiche, you know,' she said provocatively.

'I'm sure you do, but I wouldn't waste my time making it here, if I were you. The men don't like anything fancy, so keep meals plain. They do like their puddings, though, the more old-fashioned the better.'

'Right.' Meredith sighed inwardly. She had the feeling that she was going to get awfully tired of cooking beef and fruit crumble.

'There's a vegetable plot over there,' Hal went on, pointing through the window, 'but when anyone gets the chance to go to Townsville they'll bring back fruit and vegetables that we can't grow here, so we do get some variety.'

But Meredith wasn't listening. She had looked obediently in the direction Hal was pointing, but her gaze was snagged by something much more incredible than a vegetable patch. 'Is that a *lemon* tree?' she asked in delight.

'Yes,' said Hal cautiously, wondering what all the excitement was about.

'Wow!' Meredith's face was alight with pleasure. 'I've never seen one of those before. I can't wait to go and pick my own lemon!'

Hal regarded her with surprise. He hadn't expected her to be pleased by something so simple. She looked suddenly vivid and her eyes were bright with interest. They really were an extraordinary colour, he found himself thinking. A deep, dark blue, almost purple, they were eyes you could lose yourself in if you weren't careful.

'I'll show you the rest of the homestead,' he said brusquely, wrenching his gaze away.

Meredith hadn't taken in much the day before, but in daylight it was clear that the kitchen area was a relatively modern extension, while the main part of the homestead seemed to date back to the beginning of the twentieth century. It was something of a surprise to Meredith, who had been expecting everything to be as functional as the kitchen and the bedroom wing where she had slept the night before. Here, the ceilings were high, the doors solidly made and the rooms had the fine proportions of a more gracious era. How on earth had they managed to build a house like this in the middle of nowhere, without any of the benefits of modern technology?

'We don't use these rooms much,' Hal said, opening a door into an old-fashioned dining room with a beautiful antique dining table, and then into an elegant sitting room. Long windows looked out past the deep veranda to the garden and the tree-lined creek in the distance.

'Oh, this is a lovely room!' exclaimed Meredith, walking in and looking around with pleasure. 'At least, it could be if it had a good clean.' She wiped a finger along the top of a rosewood cabinet and wrinkled her nose. 'That and a fresh lick of paint and it could be wonderful.'

'It doesn't need painting,' said Hal bluntly. 'I never sit in here.'

'What a shame.' Meredith wandered over to the windows and fingered the faded curtains. 'No wonder it feels unloved. Someone must have loved this room once, though, someone with a lot of taste, by the look of it. Your mother?'

'I don't remember,' said Hal, his voice curt to the point of rudeness.

'Oh?' She hesitated, not wanting to pry, but it was odd that he didn't remember at all. 'Did you lose your mother quite young?'

'I was twelve,' he said after the tiniest of pauses.

'I was five when my mother died,' Meredith offered. 'My father remarried, though, a couple of years later.'

She looked around the tranquil room. If Hal was in his thirties now, and his mother had died when he was fourteen, this room probably hadn't been used for nearly a quarter of a century. How sad, she thought. And how strange that he didn't remember his mother sitting here.

'It doesn't look as if your father married again,' she said.

'No.'

'You can tell,' said Meredith. 'The whole house needs a woman's touch.'

'None of the housekeepers stay long, but they generally keep the place clean,' said Hal stiffly.

'It's not about dusting,' she said. 'A room like this needs someone to love it and live in it. A quick run round with a vacuum cleaner isn't going to bring it back to life!' She glanced at him curiously. 'You've never thought of getting married?'

'Once.' Hal was wishing that he hadn't brought Meredith in here. The room brought back too many memories at the best of times. Now it seemed dingier and sadder than ever in contrast to Meredith's vibrancy. 'It didn't work out.'

Now, to his dismay, she perched on the arm of a sofa, frankly interested. 'Why not?'

Hal shrugged. 'I met Jill through mutual friends in Darwin. We got on well and had a good time when we were together. I used to go up to Darwin to stay with her and she came down here a couple of times, but after we got engaged she decided to come and spend more time here.

'She only lasted a couple of weeks,' he remembered grimly. 'It made her realise how isolated her life would be if she married me, and she decided she couldn't go through with it.'

'I'm sorry,' said Meredith, wondering what Jill had been like. Was she sweet? Was she pretty? There must have been something special about her to capture a heart as hard as Hal Granger's. What did a woman have to have to get him to let down that guard and smile and laugh and love?

Not that she was interested personally. It was just intriguing to see what made people fall in love.

'Don't be.' Hal leant against the back of an armchair and crossed his long legs at the ankle. Meredith was struck anew by his physical presence. He looked strong and solid and incredibly *male* in this faded, feminine room. No wonder he never sat in here.

'At least Jill was honest,' he said. 'It was much better for her to decide that it wasn't going to work then than after we were married and might have had children to complicate matters.'

'It must have hurt, though. Rejection's never any fun,' said Meredith with feeling, but Hal only shrugged.

'It was a mutual decision. We're still friends,' he said. 'She's in Melbourne now. She married a doctor and they're very happy as far as I can tell.'

'And you haven't met anyone since?'

'No one who could deal with the isolation. No one I could face being isolated with either, come to that.'

'Don't you ever get lonely?'

'Do you?' he countered.

'Me?'

'You told me that you live on your own,' he reminded her. 'I don't. There are usually at least seven other men here and you'd be surprised how often we have other people passing through. Government inspectors, scientists, journalists, visitors, road train drivers, helicopter pilots… Sometimes there are twenty people sitting round the table in the evening. I don't get much chance to be lonely.'

'Yes, but that's not the same as having someone special,' said Meredith.

Hal cocked a brow at her. 'Are you by any chance asking what I do for sex?' he asked.

The colour rushed into Meredith's cheeks. 'Of course not!' she said, aghast.

'Because that's what it sounded like,' Hal finished, but Meredith was too embarrassed to hear the amusement threading his voice at first.

'I wouldn't dream of asking you *that*! God, of *course* not! I just meant whether you ever wanted someone…well, someone close, someone to talk to and laugh with and—'

'Sleep with?' he suggested, and this time she did hear the undercurrent of mockery.

She tilted her chin at him, refusing to rise. 'Well, *don't* you want someone like that?' she challenged him.

'Sometimes I do, but not for long,' Hal told her frankly. 'I never get involved with a woman who's looking for "commitment".' He made hooks with his fingers to emphasise his distaste for the word.

Meredith hoped she looked as if she took attitudes like that in her stride. 'And where do you find women who *aren't* looking for that?' she asked.

'We do have a social life in the outback, you know. Balls, races, rodeos, weddings and parties... You might have to travel a couple of hundred miles to get there, but you still go and you'd be surprised how many people you meet.' His eyes rested on Meredith's face, still pink with embarrassment. 'And then, of course, there are girls like you.'

'Like me?' Meredith's voice went up a notch. 'What do you mean, *like me*?'

'Like you in that they're cooks and housekeepers,' Hal explained. 'We get a very high turnover out here. Girls usually only stay two or three months, which is why I had to tie Lucy to that contract to make sure she was still here when the kids came. Often, the girls who come out want to experience outback life for a while, but they don't want to live here for ever. Sometimes we have a nice time together for a while, and then they leave with no regrets on either side.'

'I hope you're not telling me that sleeping with you is part of my duties,' snapped Meredith, who was not nearly as sophisticated as she looked, and didn't quite know how to deal with Hal's frankness. More rattled by the idea than she wanted to admit, she crossed her arms in an unconsciously defensive gesture.

'No,' said Hal. 'Not unless you wanted to, of course,' he added after a tiny pause.

'Unless I …?' Meredith leapt to her feet, hardly able to credit what she had heard. Unless she wanted to! The cheek of it!

She glared at Hal, who looked back, one eyebrow lifted as if in surprise, and she had the sudden, sickening feeling that she had over-reacted to what had probably been a joke. Tossing her head, she made a big deal of brushing down her trousers. 'Certainly not!' she said, as coolly as she could.

'I didn't think so.' Hal didn't sound particularly bothered, which perversely annoyed Meredith even more.

Presumably it had been a joke.

'You're not telling me that you would actually consider a relationship with me?'

'A temporary one,' Hal clarified. 'From my point of view, you'd be ideal. I can be sure you don't want commitment, after all. I know you can't wait to get on that plane back to England.'

Meredith was outraged. 'And so I'd do, would I? I'd be convenient for you?'

'I wouldn't put it quite like that,' said Hal, 'but if you liked the idea, I certainly wouldn't say no.'

'I can assure you that the idea has no appeal for me whatsoever!' she said in her most quelling voice.

Not that Hal seemed the slightest bit quelled. 'Well, let me know if you change your mind,' was all he said, casually uncrossing his legs and straightening from the chair. 'Shall we get on?'

Meredith could hardly believe it. The nerve of the man! He had barely smiled at her since she'd arrived and now here he was, casually suggesting they might sleep together if she felt like it!

How was she supposed to respond to something like that? Meredith wondered as she followed him out of the room. Had Hal really expected her to say, 'Oh, OK, then,' as if it were no big deal?

And if she had, then what would he have done? Would he have kissed her then, or would he have waited until later that night, when the children were in bed and the stockmen had gone back to their quarters? He might have smiled at her then. He might have drawn her to him...and what would *that* have been like?

Meredith was annoyed to find that her mouth was dry and she swallowed. How on earth had they started this stupid conversation? Now, infuriatingly, in spite of her furious efforts to keep looking straight ahead, her eyes kept skittering sideways to his hands, his mouth, his throat, and then back to his mouth, before she could wrench them back...

Yesterday they had shaken hands to seal their deal. She could remember the feel of his fingers closing around hers exactly. If that had been enough to send a secret thrill through her, what would a kiss do? What would a whole night together do?

This time, Meredith actually gulped. Stop it, she scolded herself as she stalked along the corridor beside Hal, frowning with the effort of keeping eyes and mind under control. Stop it, stop it, stop it! You said no and you meant no.

Thank God she was sensible and not impulsive like Lucy, who lived for the moment and might easily tumble into an affair like that without giving a thought to the consequences. Well, the subject was closed now. She wouldn't even *think* about it any more.

'Did you ask Lucy if she wanted to sleep with you?' she heard herself demanding.

If Hal was surprised at her abrupt question, he gave no sign of it. 'No.'

'Why not?'

'Would you believe me if I said that Lucy wasn't my type?'

'No,' said Meredith without hesitation. She had never yet met a man who didn't fall for Lucy. Hal's words implied that her dumpiness appealed to him more than Lucy's slender, golden beauty and not for a minute did Meredith believe *that*.

Hal glanced down at her. 'If you won't believe that, will you believe that Lucy fell for Kevin the moment she laid eyes on him, and after that it was obvious that none of the rest of us were in with a chance?'

'That sounds more like it,' said Meredith.

There was no way that she, rather than Lucy, would be Hal's type. Sensible girls like her were rarely anyone's type.

Meredith only just caught her sigh in time. Horrified, she gave herself a mental slap on the cheeks. It was very lucky that she was the sensible sister or she might even now be embarking on an affair with Hal Granger and what would that get her?

Excitement? a little voice inside her suggested.

It would be stupid.

It might be fun. No commitment, no strings attached, just a good time until Lucy came back and she could go home.

Excitement and fun... How long was it since she had had either? Meredith thought wistfully and then had to remind herself hastily that it wouldn't be worth it. Besides, she wasn't that kind of girl. She was practical and sensible and thought things through. She certainly wasn't going to get involved in any casual affair with Hal Granger, thrill or no thrill.

Still, it wouldn't have killed him to have seemed a bit more disappointed by her firm refusal, would it?

The last room Hal showed her was the office. 'You can work in here,' he said, opening the door into a room piled high with files and papers and magazines and alarming-looking veterinary ointments.

'How?' asked Meredith, appalled. 'You can't even see the desk for the mess!'

'Just put those papers on the floor,' he said, demonstrating with a pile. 'You can unplug the computer if you'd prefer to use your own, and the phone is in here too. There's only one line, but most people call at mealtimes when they know I'll be around, so there shouldn't be a problem.'

'How long is it since anyone tidied up in here?'

'My father wasn't much good at paperwork and I've never had time to sort it all out.'

'Right, so there's at least twenty years of junk in here?'

Hal looked round him as if seeing the office for the first time. It *had* got a bit out of hand, he supposed, but he knew where to find what he needed.

Meredith sighed and pulled the hair back from her face. 'There's no way I'm going to be able to work in a tip like this,' she said. 'But I will need to use the phone line to get on to the Internet. Can I clear things up and give it all a good clean?'

Maybe it wouldn't be a bad idea to get some order into it all. 'Knock yourself out,' said Hal. 'Just don't throw anything away without asking.'

Back in the kitchen, Hal reached for his hat. 'Think you know what you're doing?' he asked.

Meredith looked around the kitchen, piled high with dishes that Lucy hadn't had time to wash that morning, and thought of all the meals to prepare and the rest of the homestead crying out for a good clean. Where did she start? And when was she going to have five minutes to open her laptop, let alone do any work?

'It's under control,' she lied.

'Good.' Hal settled his hat on his head and opened the screen door. 'I'll leave you to it, then.'

CHAPTER FIVE

IT TOOK Meredith an hour to restore the kitchen to some semblance of order. Emma and Mickey slipped away as soon as they suspected jobs might be in the offing, but trailed back after a while, complaining that they were bored.

'You can help me make a cake if you like,' Meredith offered. She felt sorry for the poor kids, dumped out in the middle of nowhere with nothing to do and only a grim uncle and a bunch of taciturn stockmen for company. 'You choose what kind.'

'Can we make a chocolate cake?'

'You can if we can find some cocoa.' She peered into the larder, which was next on her list for a major clear out. 'I'm sure I saw some in here.'

By the time Hal came in later that morning, the cake was in the oven, Meredith had heard all about the children's lives in Sydney and the carefully tidied kitchen was once more looking as if the proverbial bomb had hit it. Emma and Mickey were licking out the cake bowl, measuring how much the other had taken with eagle-eyed precision, and Meredith was resignedly wiping up the debris when the clatter of the screen door announced Hal's arrival.

Her body was still strumming with a mixture of indignation and something that was shamefully like excitement in spite of her best efforts to work it out of her system. She had thrown herself into a frenzy of cleaning all morning, but she might as well not have bothered judging by the way her heart jerked at Hal's appearance. The strange buzzing sensation in the pit of her stomach immediately ratcheted itself up to full vibration.

It wasn't the kind of thing sensible stomachs did. Crossly, Meredith scrubbed at a sticky patch with renewed vigour.

Hal sniffed appreciatively as he hung up his hat. 'Something smells good.'

'We made a cake,' said Mickey importantly.

'It's for smoko this afternoon,' Emma added, anxious not to miss out on the glory.

'That sounds great.' Hal looked around the

kitchen and his eyes came to rest on Meredith, still rubbing industriously. 'You've been busy.'

'Just doing my job,' said Meredith, horrified to hear that her voice was positively squeaky. She rinsed out the cloth under the tap and willed her nerve endings to stop carrying on as if it were party time. Honestly, anyone would think that she was attracted to him!

Or that she wished she'd accepted his offer.

Wringing out the cloth rather more forcefully than necessary, she laid it by the sink and turned to Hal, disguising her unaccustomed nervousness in brisk practicality.

'You don't know if there's an apron around, do you?' There, that was much better. Nobody whose nerves were fluttering frantically with awareness under their skin would even be able to *think* about aprons, let alone care whether they were wearing one or not, would they? 'I couldn't find one anywhere.'

'An apron?' Hal made it sound as if she had asked for an intergalactic spaceship, and there was probably about as much chance that she would find one of *those* out here, Meredith reflected. 'What do you want an apron for?'

'Why does anyone ever want an apron? To protect my clothes, of course,' she said sharply. 'Look at the state of me!'

Hal looked. She looked fine to him. Overdressed as usual, and perhaps not as well-groomed as she might have been after this morning's trip in the back of the truck, but she was gesturing fastidiously at her front as if she'd been castrating bullocks. Hal didn't care to think how she would react to what went on in the yards. He made a mental note to keep her away from there.

'I can't lay my hands on an apron, but I could find you an old shirt,' he said. 'Would that help?'

'It would be better than nothing,' she accepted as graciously as she could.

Hal was back a few minutes later. 'It'll be too big for you,' he told her, handing her a shirt that was soft and faded from repeated washings. It had once had a blue check that now looked more like a smudgy grey. 'At least it might cover you up, though.'

'Thank you,' said Meredith, taking it from him and lifting it to her face without thinking. 'Mmm, it smells nice,' she said, breathing in the clean fragrance of sun-dried cotton and something else that she couldn't quite identify.

Hal raised an eyebrow. 'It's one of my old shirts, but it's perfectly clean. It shouldn't smell of anything.'

'I know.' Meredith flushed at the realisation that the lovely, clean but unmistakably masculine scent was Hal's. Please God he didn't guess that she had recognised it. She cleared her throat. 'I just like the smell of clean clothes,' she excused herself and then regretted it. Now she sounded like some kind of pervert who went around sniffing laundry.

'Whatever turns you on,' he said and the children sniggered. It was obvious they all thought that she was deeply weird. 'Anyway, the shirt's yours. I haven't worn it for a while and it doesn't matter how dirty you get it.'

Mortified, Meredith clutched the shirt to her chest and wished that Hal hadn't mentioned being turned on. The mere feel of the shirt in her hands was enough to make her think about how he would have looked, bare-chested, as he shrugged it on. How many times had this material rested against his skin? God, she was actually *stroking* it, she realised, appalled, and dropped it on to the table as if it had burnt her.

'Ready for smoko?' she asked crisply.

'We are, but I wasn't sure if you'd have had time to make tea.'

'Of course.' She might be sadly lacking in control on the shirt front, thought Meredith, but let no one suggest that she wasn't efficient. 'Lucy left some biscuits, so I've put them on the veranda there with some mugs. I'll just put the kettle on.'

Screened in like the dining veranda, this was the most comfortable part of the homestead where they came for smoko or to sit with a cold beer at the end of a long, hot day. It was a man's place. There were no knick-knacks or pictures or matching upholstery. Instead there were tatty wicker chairs, some limp, stained cushions and the occasional table decorated with ring marks from countless mugs and scattered with a motley assortment of magazines dating back as long as Hal could remember. No rugs, nothing fancy, just a scarred and stained concrete floor so you weren't afraid to walk in with your boots on.

At least it had been comfortable. When Hal stepped through from the kitchen, he hardly recognised it. The tables were clean, the floor shining and the chairs all lined up, the cushions plumped and realigned with military precision.

He stared around him, appalled. 'What have you done?'

'I've given it a good clean,' said Meredith as she carried in the huge teapot. 'The place was filthy.' She set the teapot on table—newly scrubbed. 'And I tidied up a bit.'

'A *bit*? This is supposed to be a place we can relax,' Hal complained. 'Now it looks as if we'll have to march in time and salute before we ask permission to sit down. What are you, woman—a frustrated sergeant major?'

'No, I'm a housekeeper,' she said tightly. 'At least, that's what I understood you wanted me to be. And housekeepers keep houses clean. This place was a tip!'

'I liked it being a tip,' said Hal, scowling. 'And what have you done with the magazines?'

'I put them in the box of papers to be incinerated.'

'What? You'd better not have burnt them!'

'Not yet, no,' Meredith admitted reluctantly, although she wished that she had now. What a fuss about a lot of old magazines!

'In that case, you can bring them back right now!'

'But they're all years out of date!' she protested.

'I don't care,' he snarled. 'Bring them back.'

'Fine.' Tight-lipped, Meredith marched out to the kitchen and retrieved the magazines. 'There you are,' she said, dumping them on a table. 'Happy now?'

'Yes,' he said grudgingly. 'Thank you.'

'Perhaps you'd better tell me where else is to be preserved as a dusty tip,' she said, her voice dripping with sarcasm. 'Or shall I assume that you don't actually want me to do any cleaning. Clearly nobody else has done any for a very long time!'

'You can clean,' said Hal, eyeing her with dislike. 'Just don't change anything.' Deliberately, he pulled a chair out of its neat line and sat down in it as the rest of the men began trooping in, all equally aghast at finding themselves somewhere clean and tidy. 'I don't like change,' he said.

Meredith drank her tea in a huff. Honestly, she fumed to herself, what was the point of having a housekeeper if you were only going to complain when she kept house? No wonder Hal

Granger had such a high turnover of cooks and housekeepers. He obviously never let them do their jobs.

The men were uneasy until they had restored the veranda to its habitual mess, which took surprisingly little time compared to how long it had taken her to clean it up, Meredith thought vengefully, but someone eventually started a conversation about something called agistment, not a word of which Meredith understood. She was heartily relieved when they all stood up to go back to work.

Still stroppy, she followed them out to where they were collecting their hats by the kitchen door. Hal was the last to go.

'What were you planning for supper?' he asked, obviously preparing to pre-empt any further disasters like them actually eating something different for a change.

'Well, let's see…' Meredith put her head on one side and pretended to consider. 'I thought I would do something simple since it's my first night,' she said, her voice dripping sarcasm. 'Perhaps filet mignon with timbales of aubergine and red pepper served with a rosemary and redcurrant coulis?'

There was a moment's silence. Deep blue eyes met cool grey in an unspoken challenge, and that should have been the end of it. But then something happened. Afterwards, Meredith couldn't really explain it to herself, but it was as if someone somewhere had flicked a switch, making the air crackle alarmingly, and she could practically see the spark jumping between them.

Whatever it was, it unnerved her enough to make her jerk her gaze away, unaccountably shaken. She moistened her lips.

'Or perhaps a bowl of mince,' she finished.

Hal settled his hat on his head in a gesture that was already familiar to her. 'Mince sounds good,' he said.

He turned to reach for the screen door, but not before Meredith had glimpsed a tell-tale dent at the corner of his mouth and that the elusive smile that never quite seemed to reach his lips was gleaming in his eyes.

The next moment he had gone, letting the door clatter shut behind him, but it was as if that smile were still there, tingling in her blood, and her huff evaporated like mist on a summer morning. To Meredith's disgust, she found herself thinking about the smile rather than about how totally un-reasonable Hal had been as she cleared the mugs from the veranda.

What on earth was the matter with her? Meredith gave herself a mental shake. She wasn't the kind of girl who went all fluttery at a smile—not that you could really call that gleam in his eye a real smile. She was a sensible, down-to-earth woman, who didn't go in for imagining sparks or smiles or anything silly like that and, even if she were, it wouldn't do her any good.

She *certainly* wasn't about to go weak at the knees for a man who was to all intents and purposes her employer. That would be a stupid thing to do, and Meredith didn't do stupid. She didn't do reckless or romantic. She did careful and considered, so that was quite enough nonsense about non-existent smiles!

No, she reminded herself, she had agreed to do this job. She didn't have to like it, she just had to get on with it. Jet lag might excuse some un-characteristic behaviour, but that was enough now. It was time to pull herself together.

And she would start off by changing into the shirt he had provided, instead of letting herself be unnerved by its scent or the fact that Hal had worn it. Pulling off her top in her bedroom, she slipped on the shirt. It felt cool and comfortable, the soft material almost caressing her skin, the way it must have caressed Hal's.

Meredith's fingers fumbled at the buttons, imagining him doing the same, imagining what it would be like if he were there now, watching her, brushing her clumsy hands aside and slowly unbuttoning the shirt with deft fingers until it slid from her shoulders.

All right! Meredith told herself fiercely as her insides promptly melted at the mere thought. She had to stop this, she had to stop it *now*. It was just a shirt and she was a sensible woman. Just do up the buttons and go and get lunch.

Being sensible didn't stop her being agonisingly aware of the feel of Hal's shirt against her body, but at least she avoided having to explain to Hal just why she had taken his shirt off after being so insistent that she wanted to protect her own clothes.

The thing is, she would have had to say to him, I keep thinking about *you* wearing it. I keep thinking about it against your bare back, and that gives me this awful, squirmy feeling in my stomach, so I decided I'd rather ruin my own clothes.

No way was Meredith having *that* conversation.

Still, it was a relief when she had supper under control that evening and could go and change into her own clothes once more. She put on a black skirt and a flattering pale blue top that hugged her curves without being too revealing, and slipped her feet into strappy sandals with vertiginous heels. Add some lipstick, and Meredith immediately felt more herself—confident and competent.

The feeling lasted until the stockmen shuffled in from their quarters for the evening meal. They had a beer on the veranda first, and stared at her as if they had never seen a woman in high heels before.

In spite of her determination not to care if she seemed out of place, Meredith was desperately self-conscious and she despised herself for it. It was true that, like Hal, the men all seemed to have showered and changed their shirts at least, but it was clear that the notion of dressing for dinner had not yet reached this part of the outback.

'You look…very…smart,' said Hal, who really

wanted to say something like *sensational* or *sexy*—or both—but thought she would probably bite his head off if he did. But those shoes…!

To Meredith, 'smart' sounded like an insult. 'I'm allowed to change in the evenings, aren't I?' she snapped. 'Or is a change of clothes too much change for you to deal with?'

Hal held up his hands. 'We're just not used to it, that's all. Lucy never changed in the evenings.'

No, well, if she had Lucy's figure and could look fabulous in jeans and a T-shirt, she probably wouldn't either, Meredith reflected with a touch of bitterness. She would love to be slender and long-legged like her sister instead of short and round. It was no surprise that people often found it hard to believe that the two of them were related. She had often wondered if there had been some mix-up at the hospital when she was born as she appeared to have no genetic connection to the rest of her family.

She didn't care anyway, Meredith reminded herself, sitting at the end of the table opposite Hal and lifting her chin defiantly. Let them think of her as strange. She didn't want to be accepted here, the way Lucy obviously had been. She didn't want to belong.

Meredith's first meal could not be said to have been a raving success. There was nothing wrong with the mince or the vegetables, all perfectly cooked, or with the apple pie she had made for pudding, but the atmosphere was distinctly awkward. Meredith was defensive, the children sullen, and Hal was having so much trouble concentrating on anything except how she looked in those shoes that he barely knew what he was eating.

Never the chattiest of company, the stockmen left immediately after pudding, leaving Meredith alone with Hal and the two children.

'What do you two do with yourselves in the evening here?' she asked Emma and Mickey, since it seemed hardly fair to them to sit in silence and she couldn't think of a thing to say to Hal, who had been looking distracted all evening.

'Nothing. It's so boring,' sighed Emma.

'There isn't even a TV,' Mickey added in the incredulous tones of a child unable to imagine anywhere without this most basic of technologies.

'There's a record player,' Hal offered in his defence, and they looked at him blankly.

'What's that?'

In spite of her determination to stay aloof, Meredith couldn't help catching Hal's eye and she smothered a smile at his expression. 'It's been a very long time since anyone played records,' she said. 'Even I never had a record player. Don't tell me you've never heard of CDs?'

'Of course I have,' said Hal. 'But, in case you hadn't noticed, music shops are few and far between out here. I just never got round to buying CDs or anything to play them on.'

'Don't you listen to music?' asked Meredith, trying to imagine a life without music. 'I always have it on in the background, even when I'm working.'

His mother had been the same, Hal remembered. There had always been music when she was around.

'I listen to the night,' he said.

Emma and Mickey exchanged a glance. Hal pushed back his chair and got to his feet, glad to get off the subject of music.

'If you two are so bored, you can come and give me a hand with the washing-up,' he said and watched their faces crumple in consternation.

'Oh, that's not *fair*!'

Meredith looked puzzled. 'I was expecting to clear up,' she said.

'No, the cook doesn't wash up the main meal,' said Hal. 'This is your time off. You can relax now and I'll bring you a cup of coffee in a minute.'

He bore the children, still protesting, off to the kitchen and Meredith was left in sole possession of the table.

Well, it was a nice idea, but what did you do with time off in a place like this? Meredith wondered. If she were at home in London, she could stretch out on the sofa and watch telly, or ring a friend and go out for a drink. She could go to a film or catch an exhibition or see if she could get a ticket to the latest play everyone was talking about.

What was there to do here? A big, fat nothing. Of course, she could do some work, but somehow the thought of going into that cheerless office—*that* was next on her list for a revamp!—and sitting at her laptop was too depressing to contemplate. Catching herself in the middle of a huge yawn as she got up from the table, Meredith reasoned that she was still suffering from jet lag and could therefore be excused from working this evening. She would get down to it tomorrow.

It was too early to go to bed, though. The children had portable DVD players, but Meredith didn't rate her chances of being able to borrow one now that they were having to wash up, and besides, she didn't think her eyes could cope with the tiny screen.

For want of anywhere else to go, she went to sit on the back veranda where she had seen that incredible sunset the day before. It was quite dark now, with no light to discourage the flying insects who hurled themselves at the blue light trap instead. Meredith was a bit disconcerted by the way it would spit and fizzle every few seconds as another insect was caught by its deadly lure.

She looked outwards instead. The night sky was quite different in the Southern Hemisphere, Meredith realised, and certainly very different from the starless yellow glow that hung above London. Here, the darkness wasn't black or grey but a deep, dark blue and blurry with brilliant white stars.

Meredith thought about Lucy, who was up in

that sky somewhere at thirty thousand feet, flying, flying, flying. The memory of that long journey made Meredith shudder. Then she thought about Richard, lying still in his hospital bed, but London seemed unimaginably distant, here in the vastness of the Australian outback. It was hard to remember exactly what Richard looked like.

Or why she had loved him so much.

Behind her, the screen door creaked, jolting her out of her thoughts, and through the dim light she saw Hal looming with two mugs.

'So this is where you are,' he said, an odd note in his voice.

'Is it OK for me to be here?'

'Of course. I was just surprised to find you here. This is where I like to sit at night too.'

'Oh.' Meredith felt as if she ought to move, but it seemed rude to leave the moment he had arrived and, besides, he had brought her coffee.

She took it with a murmur of thanks and after a second's hesitation Hal sat down in the chair next to hers. There was a table between them where she could put down her mug, but he still felt overwhelmingly close and she was suddenly reminded of how she had felt when she had put his shirt on earlier that day. The thought brought a flush to her cheeks and she was very glad of the dim light that hid her expression.

'You're not working tonight?' he asked after a moment.

'I should be,' she said, 'but I can't face it until I've cleared that desk.'

'You're entitled to sit down and do nothing for a bit. You've been working all day and it's all strange to you.'

'It's certainly that,' said Meredith ruefully.

Hal's eyes rested on her profile. In the dim light he could see little more than the pearly gleam of her skin and the outline of that lush mouth, but he could still picture exactly how she had looked as she had walked into the veranda that night in those ridiculously unsuitable and sexy shoes and announced that supper was ready. Her chin had been up at its usual combative angle and her eyes had been sharp and bright, but the rest of her was all warm curves and soft lines.

Hal pushed the memory firmly aside.

'I'm sorry, I was probably a bit abrupt with

you earlier about the veranda,' he apologised. 'I'm not very good with change.'

'I gathered that,' she said dryly.

'I'm only thirty-five, but I guess I'm set in my ways,' he said, trying to explain. 'I've lived here at Wirrindago all my life, and I've been running the station on my own for the last fifteen years. I'm used to things being a certain way.' He shrugged. 'That's probably why I'm finding the kids a bit difficult.'

'Where are they now?'

'Playing some computer game in their rooms and recovering from drying up a few dishes. You'd think holding a tea towel was a form of torture.' Hal sighed and swirled the coffee round in his mug. 'I don't understand them,' he admitted. 'I feel as if I've let them down, but I don't know what to do with them. They seem to be bored the whole time. We were never bored when we were children.'

Meredith eyed him over the rim over her mug. 'What did you used to do?'

'We used to have to help around the station, for a start,' said Hal, 'but when we'd done our jobs, we'd ride or go fishing or mess around by the creek. We'd go off exploring on our own for hours.'

His voice trailed off as he realised how long it was since he'd let himself talk about his childhood. Since he'd let himself think about it.

'That was you and Lydia?'

And Jack. Hal wasn't ready to talk about Jack.

'Yes,' he said.

Meredith drank her coffee thoughtfully. 'Maybe you should show Emma and Mickey what you used to do?' she suggested. 'After all, their mum grew up here. She must have talked about it.'

Lydia wouldn't have talked about Jack.

'Maybe,' Hal agreed. But how could he show them the creek and the rocks and the water hole and not think about Jack?

A silence fell, but it wasn't an uncomfortable one. The blue light fizzled and snapped, but above it Meredith could hear insects shrilling and the strange cracks and rustles of the darkness, and she thought about what Hal had said about listening to the night.

A creeper that looked much too exotic to survive in the British climate was climbing up the veranda post, its scent heady on the night air. In the starlight, she could see a frangipani tree, recognised from holidays in Greece, its fragrant white blooms almost glowing in the dark, but beyond that there was nothing, just an ancient, immense darkness crouching in the silence.

Meredith shivered and sipped her coffee, glad that Hal was there.

'Haven't you ever wanted kids of your own?' she asked, wanting the reassurance of his voice.

Hal's face closed. 'No.'

'Why not?'

'Why should I?'

'Well…I don't know,' she admitted. 'I suppose I'd expect you to want to pass the land on to your children. Farmers are always supposed to think in terms of generations, aren't they?'

'This farmer doesn't,' said Hal flatly. 'Wanting children means wanting a mother for those children.'

'The two usually go together,' Meredith agreed.

'I'm not going to take the risk of marrying someone and having children. There's no guarantee that the marriage would last. It's hard enough under normal conditions, but when you add in isolation and drought and all the other things you have to contend with in the outback…no.' He shook his head. 'It's not a risk I'm prepared to take.'

'There's no guarantee that a marriage wouldn't last either,' Meredith pointed out. 'Some marriages are very happy.'

'None that I know of,' said Hal.

'If I were talking to one of my friends in London, I'd say you had real commitment issues,' said Meredith with one her acerbic looks.

'What about you?' Hal countered. 'I don't see you having committed yourself to marriage either.'

'That's because I haven't met the right man yet, not because I'm afraid of commitment.'

Hal raised a brow in disbelief. 'Don't tell me you're waiting for Mr Perfect?'

'What's wrong with that?'

'Only that you strike me as a sensible woman, and it doesn't seem like a very sensible thing to do. You must know as well as I do that no one will ever be perfect, which gives you *commitment issues* too,' he said. 'Instead of admitting that you don't want to take the risk, you pretend you're waiting for someone who doesn't exist.'

'Who says he doesn't?' demanded Meredith fiercely. 'I'm not waiting for a man who's perfect, just a man who's perfect for me.'

'I can't believe a sensible girl like you would

fall for that happy-ever-after fantasy,' said Hal with a snort of contempt.

'Actually, it's a perfectly sensible approach.' Meredith's voice was cool. 'Lucy falls in and out of love the whole time, and it always seems to me that it's a waste of time and energy and emotion when any fool can see that it's not going to last. It's much more sensible to wait until you're sure that you've met someone who's going to make you happy before you let yourself fall in love.'

'But how can you tell?'

'You just can. I'm looking for someone kind and sensitive and intelligent. Someone with integrity. Someone I can talk to…a friend.'

Richard had been all those things. He was everything Meredith had ever wanted in a man, so of course she had fallen for him. It wasn't Richard's fault that he hadn't felt the same about her. He had been quite happy being friends, and she had been terrified of scaring him away by telling him how she felt.

And then he had seen Lucy, and that had been that.

Meredith sighed.

'It sounds to me as if you've got very high expectations,' Hal commented.

'That's what Lucy says. She says I'm too picky, but I think you *should* be picky when it comes to choosing someone you're going to spend the rest of your life with. It's important. You and Lucy might call it having unreasonably high expectations, but *I* call it being sensible.'

'And you're not prepared to compromise?' asked Hal, who hadn't been able to avoid noticing that her wish list for a man didn't include many characteristics that would apply to him. He hadn't been particularly kind or sensitive as far as she was concerned, he had to admit.

Meredith finished her coffee and put the mug down with a little click. 'Not on the important things,' she told him. 'I've seen lots of my friends going to enormous lengths to change themselves and their expectations when they meet a man and decide he's The One, but I've never yet seen a man changing. Women will accept that their man is unreliable or reluctant to commit because they love him. They accept being taken for granted and never being made to feel that they're special because if they didn't accept it the relationship would be over and they're afraid of that.

'They can accept that if they want to,' said Meredith, 'but I don't see why I should. I'm not perfect, far from it. I know I'm bossy and prickly and uncompromising and I'm never going to win a beauty contest, but I don't want to change, and I want a man who doesn't want me to change either. I want someone who'll love me the way I am, someone I don't feel the need to change for.' She sent Hal one of her challenging looks. 'That's sensible, isn't it?'

'If you really think you're going to meet someone who lives up to all those expectations,' he said in a sceptical voice. 'Have you ever met anyone who did?'

There was a tiny pause. Meredith watched a moth blunder into the blue light. 'Once,' she said.

'So how come it didn't work out?' asked Hal harshly, unaccountably irritated by the idea of Meredith finding someone so perfect.

So unlike him.

'Or wasn't he so perfect after all?'

'No, he was perfect,' said Meredith. 'It turned out that I wasn't perfect for him, that's all. But that's OK,' she went on composedly. 'Maybe there's someone else out there for me, but until I meet him I'm not going to waste my time on anyone less than perfect.'

'You mean like me?' said Hal, hoping that he sounded suitably amused instead of chagrined.

'Yes, like you,' she said. 'As you pointed out yourself, I'm a sensible woman and that really *wouldn't* be a sensible thing to do.'

CHAPTER SIX

IT MIGHT not be sensible but at least it would be something to do, Meredith thought the next morning as she carried a bucket of scraps out to the chickens, who had a large fenced run on the far side of the yard. Spotting her, they came rushing to meet her, ruffling their feathers and tumbling over in their haste.

What was she *doing* here? Meredith wondered. All those qualifications had got her to this point, tossing scraps to chickens in the middle of the Australian outback. The heat was crushing. Shaking out the bucket, she left the chooks to it and closed the gate behind her, walking slowly back across the yard, not at all charmed by the chickens or the dogs chained up in the shade.

It was too hot and there were too many flies. She waved them irritably from her face. It must be hundreds of miles to the nearest bar. The pub at Whyman's Creek didn't count. She was thinking of somewhere cool and smart where she could sit back and enjoy a frosted glass of white wine.

Here, there was just…nothing. Miles and miles and miles of nothing beneath the glaring sky. Nothing to do, no one to talk to, if one didn't count Emma and Mickey, who could rarely be persuaded to lift their heads up from their computer games. The air was filled with the raucous cawing of crows, their cries falling mournfully into the thrumming silence.

She had been up since five to prepare breakfast. It had been a silent meal, but that was hardly surprising at that hour. Even so, Meredith had been uncomfortably aware of Hal. She had spent far more time than was necessary last night reminding herself how sensible she was in not getting involved with him.

She *was* attracted to him—Meredith was never less than honest with herself—but she simply couldn't account for it. Hal wasn't her type at all.

Richard was the kind of man she had always been attracted to, and Hal was nothing like him. Richard had twinkling brown eyes and a lovely smile. Hal's eyes were keen and hard, his smile elusive, but he had a mouth that for some reason dried the breath in Meredith's throat whenever her eyes rested on it.

Richard was charming and sensitive and not afraid to talk about his feelings. Hal was cool and self-contained. In fact, when he wasn't there, Meredith could almost persuade herself that she didn't *really* find him that attractive, but all he had to do was walk through that screen door and take off his hat and her heart would perform sickening somersaults while every sense in her body tautened as if she were walking a tightrope. Yes, thought Meredith wryly, her body was a regular circus routine when Hal was around.

Still, that was no reason to fall into bed with him. Hal belonged in this strange, red land under this immense sky and she...well, she didn't.

Meredith looked around her. Overlooked by the kitchen, the dusty yard was shaded by a big gum-tree, where the dogs drowsed in the shade, and framed by an odd assortment of outbuildings, whose purpose was obscure, at least as far as Meredith was concerned. There were a couple of huge water tanks, the chicken run and a rickety wind tower, its arms unmoving in the still, shimmering heat. To Meredith, city girl incarnate, it was all profoundly alien.

Australia was so big it was almost scary. The space and the light were so overwhelming that she was afraid that she would lose herself, crushed by the heat and the eerie silence. Meredith could practically feel herself diminishing, and she didn't like it. She liked to be in control of things, but how could she control this huge, wild place?

She had hardly given Lucy or Richard a thought either, she had realised guiltily last night. The sense of urgency that had possessed her since Richard's accident had deserted her since she had arrived at Wirrindago. She really must check her email. Lucy had promised that she would let her know when she was safely back in London.

Swinging the empty scrap bucket, Meredith climbed the steps to the kitchen with a renewed sense of purpose. It was high time she set up her computer and got down to some work too. It would be easier then to remember who she was and what she was doing here.

But she had to clean that office first. If she

opened her laptop in there now it would be choked in dust in five minutes. There was no way she could work in that mess. Hal would probably have a fit, but she didn't care. It wouldn't kill him to have one tidy room.

With everything under control in the kitchen, Meredith rolled up her sleeves and prepared to get dirty. The desk was piled so high with papers that she could hardly see the phone, and the desktop computer was shrouded in dust. She wiped it down, unimpressed. She had seen more up-to-date technology in a museum. Thank God she had brought her laptop with her.

Fine red dust lay in thick layers over everything. Meredith's eyes were soon watery from sneezing, and she was very glad of Hal's shirt which, disturbing or not, kept the worst of the dirt from her own clothes. She would have to borrow another so that she could wash this one.

Mindful of Hal's reaction to her removal of the old magazines from the veranda yesterday, Meredith was careful not to throw anything away, but she tidied and straightened and did her best to put everything in date order. Methodically, she worked through pile after pile of assorted papers and, in spite of not knowing anything about station business, she thought she did a pretty good job of sorting it out. Everything that looked similar she stacked together in date order, her eyebrows climbing as she saw some papers going back twenty-five years. Didn't these people understand the notion of filing?

It was the kind of job that appealed to Meredith's organised nature and, although she tutted, she secretly enjoyed restoring order. When it was tidy, the office would be a great place to work, she decided. On a corner, it had one window that looked out over the kitchen yard and another with a view of the garden and the lemon tree she had been so thrilled to see. A bright pink bougainvillaea scrambled over a pergola built into the garden, keeping the room cool and shady without cutting out too much of the light, and it was very quiet.

Yes, she could happily work here, Meredith thought.

She was sitting on the floor, sorting through an old cardboard box which had clearly functioned as a rudimentary filing drawer, when Hal came in, and her heart promptly began its usual impression of a trapeze artist.

Look! Up it soared into the air to perform—gasp!—a triple somersault before catching on to a pair of ankles just in time and—yes!—managing a neat flip before settling into a breathless swing from one side of her chest to another.

Desperately hoping that her internal acrobatics didn't show in her face, Meredith did her best to keep her expression cool. 'Hi,' she said, delighted at how casual she sounded.

Hal was staring suspiciously around the office. 'What are you doing in here?'

'I'd have thought that was obvious,' she said. 'I'm tidying up. You told me I could,' she reminded him before he could object. '"Knock yourself out", you said. And you don't need to panic,' she added, correctly interpreting his expression of dismay. 'I haven't thrown anything away! But there is a pile of stuff over there that looks like complete junk to me.' She pointed. 'Since you're here, could you please check it and take out anything you want to keep? The rest is going in the incinerator.'

'I'll never be able to find anything again!' grumbled Hal, but he didn't actually tell her to put everything back as he had done the day before.

Encouraged, Meredith scrambled to her feet. 'Nonsense, you've got a system now,' she said and showed him how she had arranged things into piles. 'You know, if you invested in a couple of decent filing cabinets, you could get all this stuff out of the way.'

Hal's down-turned mouth showed how much he thought of that suggestion, but he did pick up the first few papers from the junk pile and flicked through them briefly before tossing them aside. 'They can be burnt.'

Just as Meredith had thought, in fact.

Hal picked up another sheaf of papers. 'Why are you so determined to reorganise me?' he asked.

'It's nothing to do with you,' Meredith pointed out astringently. 'I can't work in the kind of mess this office was in. I wanted to use the computer to check my email in case Lucy had been in touch, but it took me an hour just to find the keyboard! A tidy office is just a bonus for you. You ought to be grateful.'

'Funnily enough, grateful is not what I feel when I find my home is being turned upside down,' said Hal, discarding another handful, but he wasn't really cross.

The truth was that he didn't really know *how* he felt. It certainly wasn't grateful. When he saw her sitting on the floor, her face smudged with dirt, with those dark, beautiful eyes and that curving mouth and his shirt caressing her generous curves…no, grateful wasn't the word.

He couldn't get used to how someone who looked so warm and soft and sexy could so often sound so tart and be so briskly competent. It made for an arresting combination and Hal wished that he hadn't blown it yesterday by so casually suggesting a temporary relationship to her. He had handled it badly, but he had been thrown as ever by the disjunction between the way Meredith looked and the way Meredith actually was.

He found her exasperating and intriguing and seductive and sometimes downright infuriating. She was interfering and managing and uncompromising, but…he liked her, Hal realised. He liked her intelligence and her sharp tongue. He liked the combative lift of her chin and the challenge in her eyes and the way she rolled up her sleeves and got on with what had to be done. He liked coming into the homestead and finding her there, her mouth turned down in disapproval at the state of things. Look at him now, coming to find her on the flimsiest of pretexts when he should still be out in the yards.

It was all a bit unexpected. Hal had been prepared to dismiss her as a shallow city girl. He had wanted to disapprove of her—and in lots of ways he *did*—but the liking had crept up on him in spite of everything she did that infuriated him, in spite of the fact that they had absolutely nothing in common.

Hal couldn't help thinking that the next few weeks would be a lot easier if he didn't like her.

'Did you hear from Lucy?' he asked, feeling the fool that Meredith obviously thought him.

Meredith nodded. 'Yes, just a quick message to say that she had arrived, but she hasn't been to see Richard yet. She seems to be staying with Guy.' There was a crease between her brows as she sat down on the revolving chair by the desk and bit her lip. 'That's my fault.'

'Why?' Hal's voice was unnecessarily harsh, but he had to distract himself somehow from the way she was chewing her lip, unaware of the effect it might be having on anyone else. Him, for instance.

'I completely forgot to give her the keys to my house.'

'I still don't understand why it's your fault.'

'Well…because Lucy hasn't got anywhere else to stay in London,' Meredith explained. 'She gave up the house she was sharing when she left for Australia. I had it all planned that Lucy could stay in my house, and now she can't.'

'Will Lucy be saying that it's her fault that she forgot to ask you for the key?' asked Hal.

'No…probably not,' she admitted reluctantly.

'Why do you assume that Lucy can't do anything for herself?'

'I don't!'

'Lucy would have organised her own flight if you and Guy had let her,' Hal said. 'She's perfectly capable, but you treat her like a child.'

Meredith bridled. 'I do *not*!'

'Don't you? I'm not surprised that Lucy wanted to come out to Australia and live her own life,' he said in the same hard voice, 'and you can't even let her do that on her own.'

'That's rubbish!' Meredith pushed her hair angrily away from her face, leaving another smear of dust on her cheek. 'I wouldn't be here if it wasn't for Richard's accident.'

'Yes, and whose idea was it to come and get

her to go back? Who made sure it happened, even when Lucy didn't particularly want to go?'

Hal didn't know why he was pushing her so hard. He had a nasty feeling it was to punish her in some way for always taking charge, for leaving him out of control, and he regretted it when he saw that Meredith was staring at him, appalled, the violet blue eyes clouded with distress.

'Is that how it seems?' she said, and her voice sounded suddenly small.

Hal felt terrible. He wanted to take back what he had said, but he couldn't, not now. 'Lucy can look after herself, you know, Meredith,' he said more gently.

'I know, it's just…' Meredith sighed, realising too late how controlling she had been. Poor Lucy. Had she really come all the way to Australia to get away from her? It was a horrible thought.

'I suppose I've always been used to looking after her,' she said slowly, trying to explain. 'I was always big sister, and she was little sister, and she felt like my responsibility, especially when we had to go to boarding school.' Her mouth twisted at the memory. 'Lucy was only seven, poor little kid.'

Hal hooked a stool out with his foot and sat down on it, leaning forward to rest his elbows on his knees. 'How old were you?'

'Nine.'

Nine. The same age as Emma. She had just been a little girl. 'You were a poor little kid too, then,' he said.

Meredith half smiled. 'I can see that now, but at the time I felt much older than Lucy. I just knew that I had to look after her.'

'You were a bit young for boarding school, weren't you?' he said curiously. 'We had to go away to school too, but not that early.'

'It was just the way things worked out.' She straightened the edges of a pile of bills on the desk. 'My father worked for an oil company and he was often posted overseas in places that weren't suitable for children. He remarried a few years after our mother died and under-standably our stepmother didn't want to stay at home with two small children who weren't even her own, so the next time he was posted she went with him and Lucy and I were sent away to school.'

Hal frowned. 'That must have been hard for

you. You can't have been very pleased when your father remarried.'

'I just accepted it. I was only five when my mother died and I don't really remember her, to tell you the truth. I've got an impression of her more than anything else...her perfume, how thrilled I was when she used to come in and kiss us goodnight when she was all dressed up to go out. We've got some photos, though, and we know that she loved us. That means a lot.

'And Fay isn't a wicked stepmother,' she told Hal. 'She really loves Dad, and she's a great expatriate wife. We'd go out in the holidays—we used to like travelling as unaccompanied minors—or she and Dad would come back to the UK, and she was always nice to us. It's not like we had a tragic life or anything.'

Maybe not, but Hal didn't think that losing your mother at five and being sent away to school at nine sounded like much of a childhood either.

'It can't have been much fun going to boarding school at that age,' he said, and Meredith grimaced.

'No, it was terrible at first,' she agreed, her hands stilling at last. 'I didn't really understand what was happening. I mean, they'd told us about school, and I thought it sounded quite exciting until I realised that my father was actually going to go away and leave us there. I thought we were going on a visit and then we'd be able to go home with him.'

She smiled sadly at her childish innocence. 'I was about to get into the car when my father told me I had to stay. He said I had to be a good girl and not cry, as I had to look after Lucy for him...so that's what I did.' She gave a little sigh, remembering. 'I guess that's what I've been doing ever since.'

'Poor kid,' said Hal quietly. He had hated being sent away to school at twelve and he knew how desolate it could feel when you were left on your own.

'I'll never forget watching my father drive away that day,' said Meredith. 'I can still feel Lucy's sticky little hand in mine and wishing I could let it go and run after him. I kept telling myself that he'd stop and turn round and tell us it was all a mistake, but it wasn't. He didn't come back.' She shook her head with pity for her smaller self.

'Lucy was crying. She didn't understand what

was happening either, and all I could do was hold on to what my father had told me. So I kept telling her that everything would be all right, and that I'd look after her. And I didn't let myself cry, in case that upset her even more.'

Hal's throat ached at the thought of the sturdy little girl, abandoned in a strange place, holding on to her little sister, her mouth trembling with the effort of not crying.

'I'm sorry,' he said.

'Oh, don't be.' Embarrassed at having fallen into something very close to self-pity, Meredith was once more all briskness. 'It wasn't so bad.' She made the bills into a neat pile and put them to one side before pulling a set of incomprehensible veterinary notes towards her. 'We got used to it eventually, and in lots of ways it was easier for me because I had Lucy to look after. I was so busy making sure that she was OK that I didn't have time to think about myself.'

She glanced at Hal. 'I can cope with anything as long as I have something to do,' she told him, 'but yes, you're probably right. I do look after Lucy too much. It's second nature now. We used to fly out to see our father and stepmother in the holidays and it was always me that had to think about tickets and getting to the airport on time when we were old enough to travel unaccompanied.'

'No wonder you're so sensible now,' he said, returning to his own task of going through the junk pile.

'I sometimes wish I could be reckless and interesting and exciting,' she confessed, 'but I just can't be.'

Hal thought she had looked pretty exciting in the high heels she had worn the night before, but decided he had better not say so.

'Do you ever try?' he asked instead.

'Of course not,' said Meredith primly. 'I'm much too sensible for that!'

They both laughed, then both realised at the same time that it had been a mistake to let their eyes meet like that. The air was suddenly tight between them and there didn't seem to be enough oxygen in the room to breathe properly.

So much for being sensible! With an effort, Meredith wrenched her eyes away from Hal's and concentrated on taking a proper breath, something that had never presented her with any difficulties before.

Mindlessly, she tidied another pile of papers and sought desperately for something to say to break the fizzing tension. Her gaze skittered around the room, resting on anything except Hal, falling at last on the creased photograph that she had pulled out of the cardboard box earlier and propped against the computer. Meredith reached for it, seizing on the change of subject.

'Talking of being children, I meant to ask you about this,' she said, swinging round on the chair and leaning forward to show him the picture without actually meeting his eyes. 'It's a lovely photo. Is that you on the right?'

The lingering smile was wiped from Hal's face. 'Where did you get that?'

His voice was like a lash and Meredith jerked back in surprise. She had wanted to change the atmosphere, but she hadn't counted on such spectacular success. The temperature in the room had plummeted and when she looked at Hal's expression she felt suddenly cold. What had she done?

Puzzled, she looked down at the photo. What was there in it to provoke such a reaction? It was just a happy family shot.

'In that box,' she said, pointing. 'There was a load of rubbish in there, but I couldn't throw it away. I thought Emma and Mickey might like to see their mum as a little girl. I presume that's her in the middle?' She tried a smile to lighten the atmosphere. 'And who's the little boy with the cheeky grin? I didn't realise— what are you *doing*?'

Her voice rose and she snatched the picture back from Hal, who had reached over to take it and was about to tear it in half.

'You can't do that!' she said, holding the photo protectively and staring at him in disbelief.

'I don't want it.' She had never seen his expression that cold. 'It's just junk.'

'But it's your family!'

'Look, it's none of your business!' Hal lost control of his temper. 'It doesn't matter who it is or what it is. It's nothing to do with you.' He glared at her. 'Why can't you just leave things alone?'

'But—'

'You could have cleared a space for your computer and got on with your own work,' he went on furiously. 'But no! You couldn't do anything as simple as that, could you? You always have to interfere. You have to poke around in things that don't concern you,' he said, practically spitting.

Shaken by his anger, Meredith moistened her lips. 'I've obviously touched a nerve,' she said carefully, still not really understanding what she had done.

'Too right you have!' Suddenly needing only to get out, Hal swung for the door. 'Keep the bloody photo if it matters so much to you,' he snarled, kicking the stool out of his way. 'But don't show it to me again. I don't want it.'

Meredith sat very still after he had gone. She heard the screen door slam and the angry clatter of his boots down the kitchen steps. Seconds later he appeared striding across the yard, his body rigid. Watching him through the window, Meredith bit her lip as he disappeared in the direction of the paddock where the horses were kept. This was her fault.

Carefully, she smoothed out the crumpled photo. It showed a family squinting at the camera, like thousands of other families before them. The man looked so like Hal that he had to be his father, so that, thought Meredith, turning her attention to the woman, had to be his mother. She had been a beautiful woman and obviously very stylish. Meredith could imagine her in that sitting room, if not in the kitchen or on the scruffy veranda.

Hal looked about twelve, so his mother must have died not long after the picture had been taken. Was that what had upset him so much?

Meredith sighed as she stared down at the faces, their smiles frozen in time. Hal was right. It was none of her business and she shouldn't have poked around in his private papers, but it had seemed such a happy picture. She had never dreamt that he wouldn't be glad to see it.

He had listened so sympathetically when she had been talking about her childhood, too. Meredith had found herself talking easily, and it had almost been like finding a friend. Now she had spoilt everything.

Depressed, she looked at her watch and got to her feet when she saw the time. She would apologise to Hal later, and would just have to hope that it wasn't too late. In the meantime, there were potatoes to be peeled.

She left the photo by the computer. It wasn't

hers to keep. If Hal wanted to destroy it, that was his choice, but she wouldn't tear it up for him.

Meredith hoped all evening for a chance to tell Hal how sorry she was, but they were never alone and she knew better than to raise the subject with anyone else there. Emma and Mickey had taken to hanging around in the kitchen, and by the time Meredith had changed into her evening clothes, the stockmen were having a beer with Hal.

Hal himself had recovered his temper, but Meredith could see that he was withdrawn and the grey eyes were shuttered. When he turned down her offer to help with the clearing up after the meal, she decided that it might be better to leave it. If Hal didn't want to talk, she shouldn't make him. For once, she *wouldn't* interfere or do what she thought was best, she thought, remembering how his comments about the way she treated Lucy had stung.

Instead, she would do some work.

The office was less inviting at night. Meredith tried to ignore the blank black windows and set up her laptop, averting her eyes from the photograph that had caused so much trouble that afternoon. Downloading her emails meant unplugging the phone, plugging in her laptop and dialing the Internet, a long process that had her remembering broadband at her house in London with affection.

She was just plugging the phone in once more when the door opened and Hal came in with a mug of coffee for her. 'I thought you'd like this if you're going to work,' he said.

'Oh…thank you.' Having waited all evening for a chance to talk to him, Meredith found herself suddenly tongue-tied.

She could see the photo still propped against the base of the desktop computer and wished that she had put it away. It felt as if there were a flashing neon arrow pointing at it, reminding Hal of her interference. She went to sit back on the chair, where her body would partly obscure the picture, but it was too late. Hal had already seen it.

'Hal, I'm sorry—' she began, but he interrupted her.

'No, I'm the one that's sorry,' he said. 'I overreacted earlier. I haven't seen a picture of my mother for over twenty years. I thought my father had destroyed them all and it was a shock to suddenly see her again.'

He took a breath, knowing that it would be impossible to explain to Meredith just how much of a shock it had been to come face to face with the past without warning like that. 'I took it out on you,' he said. 'I'm sorry.'

'I shouldn't have been looking through your papers,' Meredith apologised in her turn. 'You were right; it was none of my business.'

'I've never looked in that box,' he told her. 'It must have been my father's.'

Reaching past Meredith, Hal picked up the photograph and stood looking down at it, his mouth twisted. 'I wonder why he kept this.'

It seemed obvious to Meredith. 'It's a lovely picture.' She hesitated. 'Your mother was very pretty.'

'Yes, she was that,' Hal agreed bitterly.

'Why would your father destroy all pictures of her?' asked Meredith. The pictures she and Lucy had of their own mother were their most treasured possessions. 'It seems a terrible thing to do.'

'As terrible as destroying a family?' Hal dropped the picture back on the desk. 'That's what she did.'

'Your *mother*?' she said, startled. 'But...I thought she died.'

'No, she didn't die,' said Hal, a muscle beating in his clenched jaw. 'She's alive and well and living in Sydney, apparently. I haven't seen her since she walked away from Wirrindago when I was twelve. She didn't even say goodbye. She just left Dad a note, got into the ute and drove herself to Whyman's Creek one day. Dad had to go and collect it from the airport after she'd gone.'

Meredith stared at him, shocked. 'She abandoned you?'

'She abandoned us all. Lydia was only nine.'

The same age she had been when she had been left at boarding school, Meredith thought. She had felt abandoned then, but what if it had been her own mother who had walked out on her? Meredith couldn't imagine it. She couldn't imagine leaving her own children.

'Jack was ten,' he went on, and she remembered the little boy with the cheeky grin.

'Your brother?'

'Yes,' said Hal, but he didn't elaborate.

'Do…do you know why she went?' she asked after a moment.

'Oh, yes,' he said with a grim smile. 'She was bored.'

'Bored?'

Hal raised an eyebrow at her incredulous expression. 'I would have thought that you of all people would understand. You're a city girl too. You don't like the heat and the flies and the loneliness.'

'No,' Meredith agreed, stung by the implication that she would understand walking out on a family. 'But I'm not married to you and I don't have three children!'

'True,' he conceded. He leant back against the desk and picked up the picture once more, holding it as if he were fascinated and yet hated it at the same time. 'Well, it was too much for my mother.'

He studied his mother's face. He had forgotten how young and pretty she had been. 'She should never have married my father in the first place. She was from Brisbane. They met at some outback ball and she fell in love with the idea of living on a cattle station, but year after year of the reality of it wore her down. Some years can be hard,' he told Meredith. 'She missed having friends and complained that my father and the men only talked about cattle and horses, which they probably did.'

'But what about you? Her children?' Meredith was still struggling with the idea that anyone could walk away from their children. 'Didn't she want you to go with her?'

Hal glanced up at her then, his grey eyes hard with the memory. 'We would have cramped her style,' he said. 'She'd been going on longer and longer visits to her family, which turned out to be just a cover for meeting up with an old boyfriend. They moved to Sydney together—got married eventually—and they wouldn't have wanted three half-wild kids around. Besides,' he said, 'we wouldn't have gone. We couldn't imagine living in a city. Wirrindago was all we knew.'

Meredith was silent. It was easier to understand now why Hal was so determined not to get married. He wasn't prepared to take the risk of being abandoned again, the way he had been as a boy.

'It must have been very hard for you all,' she said after a while. 'How did your father cope?'

'Badly.'

'And you?' she asked gently.

Hal's eyes went back to the picture, but this time he wasn't looking at his mother. He was looking at the children with their bright, confident faces, unclouded by any suspicion that the world they knew could ever end.

'We thought we were OK,' he said. 'After Mum left, Dad let things slip, and we were allowed to do what we wanted. For a while it was almost like a holiday.'

He remembered those days so clearly. The freedom they had once longed for had been terrifying now, but they'd stayed out as long as they could, finding more and more dangerous things to do because they hadn't wanted to go home. They hadn't wanted to see the expression in their father's eyes, or think about the empty place at the table where their mother had sat. She had been away often, as he had told Meredith, but this time her absence had been like a cold, heavy stone in his stomach.

'You must have missed her,' said Meredith. Children were programmed to adore their mothers, however little they might deserve it.

'I suppose we did,' Hal said slowly. 'Jack certainly did. He'd been her favourite. He never talked about it, but I don't think he ever got over the way Mum left without saying goodbye to him. He thought that if he could just go and find her, he could make her come back and everything would be all right again.' Hal's face twisted. 'He was only a kid. He didn't know.'

At the look on Hal's face, dread began to pool in Meredith's stomach. 'What happened?' she whispered.

'One day he ran away to try and find her. He had a plan, he said. He left a note and everything.' Hal's voice was very bleak, very controlled. 'He sneaked on to a road train. The driver didn't have a clue until they unloaded and found his body in with the cattle. They think he suffocated.'

CHAPTER SEVEN

THERE was a long, terrible silence. 'Oh…Hal…' Meredith didn't know what to say.

Hal acknowledged her sympathy with a hunch of his shoulders. 'You see why Dad didn't want any reminders of her around? After Jack…I'll never forget the way he tore up every picture, anything that might remind us of her. He wouldn't have her name mentioned, and we all pretended that she was dead. Like Jack.'

'Did your mother know?'

'She must have done. I don't know if she ever tried to contact Lydia or me—if she did, Dad wouldn't have told us. Lydia's seen her once or twice in Sydney, but I've never wanted to, not after Jack, and not after what she did to my father.'

He shook his head. 'Dad was never the same after she left. I think there was part of him that knew it had been inevitable from the start, and that they should probably never have got married in the first place, but still, he couldn't break himself of her spell. After she left, he just...gave up. He lost interest. It was only when he died that I realised how far he had let Wirrindago run down. It's taken a long time to build things up again.'

Meredith's throat was tight as she watched Hal, trying to imagine life in the homestead over twenty years ago, when his mother had gone and Jack was dead and his father had turned in on himself. Her heart ached for him, for the boy he had been, and she wanted to take him in her arms and hold him tightly.

'I'm sorry,' she said instead, desperately conscious of how inadequate that sounded.

Hal looked into her warm, dark eyes and felt something tight around his heart loosen. 'That's what I said to you when you told me about boarding school, and you told me that you got used to it,' he reminded her. 'It was the same for me.'

'Who looked after you and Lydia?'

'We ran pretty wild for a time, then my father's sister got wind of the situation and came to sort us out. She'd grown up at Wirrindago but met

Guy's father when she was in England and stayed there. She and my father were always close, and I think she hated seeing how broken he was by what had happened, but she's a very practical person too. In fact, you remind me of her a lot,' Hal said with a half smile.

'She arranged for a housekeeper and tried to get us back to our schooling. I went to boarding school and she took Lydia to live with her in England until she was old enough to go to boarding school as well.'

Meredith hated the thought of Hal, losing his mother and his brother, and then his little sister too before being sent off to school on his own. Poor boy.

'Going to boarding school must have been horrible for you,' she said compassionately.

'No worse than for you,' said Hal, 'and I was nearly thirteen, not nine.'

'I had Lucy,' she pointed out. He hadn't had Jack or Lydia.

But Hal refused to be pitied. 'It was the right decision. I missed Wirrindago, but at least I got some education, and it was easier for Dad not to have to worry about who was looking after Lydia and me. I'd come back in the holidays and once a year my aunt would come out, bringing Lydia and Guy with her.'

'So that's why you're so close to Guy?'

He nodded. 'Guy was like another brother for me and Lydia. It wasn't that he replaced Jack, but we didn't miss Jack so badly when he was there. He was always fun.'

Meredith's memory of the evening she had arrived was somewhat hazy, but she still had a clear impression of Guy's dancing eyes and the way Hal had laughed with him. Guy must have been very good for Hal and his sister.

'What about Lydia?' she asked. 'Are you still close to her?'

'I'd say so. I suppose I feel responsible for her, and Lydia's quite capable of taking advantage of that. You see,' he added, 'I'm in no position to criticise you and Lucy!'

'Is that why you agreed to look after Emma and Mickey?'

'It's certainly why I feel guilty about not giving them a better time.' Hal rubbed his face. 'I think you're right. I should take them out and show them what we used to do when we were kids.'

His eyes took on a faraway expression as he remembered. 'We had some good times.'

'You should remember those.' Meredith got up and picked up the photo from the desk. 'Maybe your father remembered them too,' she said. 'Maybe that's why he kept this.

'You all look so happy,' she said, looking down at the picture. 'Jack's there, and your mother. He must have wanted something to remind him that it hadn't all been bad. You have to believe that however terrible things are, there have been times when it was all worth it; otherwise it would be too hard to bear.'

She hesitated and then held out the photo. 'You should keep this picture, Hal,' she said. 'Don't tear it up. Keep it and remember what you had, not what you lost.'

There was such a long pause while Hal just looked at the picture that Meredith lost her nerve. 'I'm sorry,' she said. 'I shouldn't have said anything; it's not my business. And I'm sorry if I brought back bad memories today. I should have left the office alone.'

'No,' said Hal abruptly and took the photo from her. 'I was angry earlier, but now I'm glad that you did find it. I haven't talked about Jack for years, and maybe I should have done.'

He put the picture in the breast pocket of his shirt. 'That coffee's cold,' he said, nodding down at her mug. 'Want another one?'

Meredith shook her head with a smile, tacitly accepting the change of subject. 'I'm used to drinking cold coffee.'

Hal straightened from the desk. 'I'd better leave you to get on with some work,' he said, and started to head for the door before changing his mind. He stopped and turned back to her.

'Thank you for tonight, Meredith,' he said quietly.

'I didn't do anything.'

'I think you did,' he said. He couldn't bring himself to say more about what it had meant to talk about Jack again, but she must have understood. She looked at him with compassion in her dark blue eyes.

'In that case, I'm glad it helped,' she said and, on an impulse that took her by surprise as much as him, she reached out and hugged him.

For a moment Hal tensed, then his arms came round her and he held her tight, as tight as a twelve-year-old boy who had lost his mother and his brother might have clung to comfort.

But this was no twelve-year-old. This was the body of a man in his prime, and it was wonderfully solid. Meredith rested her face against his shoulder and allowed herself the luxury of being held for once. His back was broad and firm, and warm beneath her hands.

'Thank you for telling me about Jack,' she murmured into his neck. Her face was very close to his throat. She could see the prickle of stubble, the steady pulse beneath his ear, and she was gripped by a longing to touch her lips to it, to taste his skin, to kiss her way along that firm jaw to his mouth.

She really mustn't do that, though. She absolutely mustn't. This was supposed to be a friendly hug, nothing else. It was just that he smelt so good, that he *felt* so good, so lean, so strong, so safe.

'I'm glad you know.'

When Hal spoke Meredith could feel his deep voice vibrating through her. His cheek was resting on her hair. It would be so easy to turn her face just a little more, to tip it up so he could find her mouth with his.

Do it! Do it! her senses urged her. Look how close he's holding you! He won't mind. You can kiss him if you want to. He'll kiss you back, and you don't need to stop. You can tug his shirt out from his jeans and run your hands over his back and find out if it's as smooth and solid as it feels. And, if you do that, he'll pull you even tighter against him. His lips will be warm and sure, you know they will. His kisses will be hot and slow, his hands hard—

Oh, God, she had to stop this *right now*! Aghast at how near she had come to letting her fantasies lead her astray, Meredith swallowed hard and, with a superhuman effort, pulled herself away like the sensible woman she was.

Her body was clamouring with disappointment, her cheeks burning, and her eyes slid away from his. She couldn't meet that grey gaze and realise that he had known *exactly* what she'd been thinking as she'd clung to him.

It was very lucky that she had never taken up counselling, Meredith told herself as she fumbled her way back to her chair. She would be struck off. It simply wasn't fair to pretend to be a friend, to let a man tell you about the childhood experiences that had scarred him, and then jump him to make yourself feel better. Meredith cringed at how close she had come to doing just that.

From somewhere she produced a bright smile. 'I must get on with some work,' she said, still without meeting his eyes.

'Of course.' After the slightest hesitation, Hal moved to the door. 'I'll leave you to it. Goodnight, Meredith,' he said, and then he was gone.

'How would you kids like to go swimming this afternoon?'

It was the following Saturday, and the stockmen had left to finish their jobs that morning. They were free after lunch until Monday and had been discussing plans for the weekend over breakfast. Meredith had gathered that they would all be going to the pub in Whyman's Creek as usual and would spend the night there.

Which meant she would be alone with Hal and the children.

She had been at Wirrindago over a week now, a week in which she had grown accustomed to so much that had seemed strange when she'd first arrived. Cooking steak at five in the morning while the homestead was still dark and cool, listening to the clatter of boots as the men came up the steps, walking through the shimmering heat to feed the chickens...even the creak of the screen door was so familiar to her now that she hardly noticed it. She was used to the vast sky and the brilliant light and the echoing silence, broken only by the cawing of crows and the occasional squabble of corellas down by the creek.

It was only Hal she couldn't get used to. The circus antics of her heart whenever he walked in the door still left her breathless. She wasn't used to the clutch of her entrails when he turned or smiled or simply put on his hat, or the warm feeling that would steal up from her stomach and start to shiver somewhere just below her skin whenever she thought about how it had felt to hold him.

Lucy had emailed with the good news that Richard was out of the coma, but still very ill. She had written:

But you were wrong about it being me he really wanted to see. He's been really sweet about it, but he told me yesterday that he'd already realised before the accident that he was over me. Still, I'll stay until I know he's definitely on the mend.

Meredith was puzzled to hear about Richard's apparent change of heart and she couldn't help wondering if Lucy was telling her everything that was going on, but there didn't seem to be much she could do about it out here. More worrying was just how glad she was to discover that her sister wasn't coming back just yet.

And that was in spite of working harder than she ever had before. Meredith had always been a hard worker, but she had never worked like this. She was up early to cook breakfast every morning, and she barely stopped until she sat down at her laptop after supper to do the equivalent of another day's work. She wasn't getting as much done as when she'd been at home, of course, but she was still on top of things.

It was lucky that she thrived on being busy, Meredith reflected, or she would be on her knees. Sometimes she did think that it would be nice just to sit down at the end of the day, but she never allowed herself to consider that as an option for too long. It would mean sitting alone in the dark with Hal, and Meredith didn't trust herself to do that.

Something very strange was happening to her. When Hal was there, she couldn't take her eyes off his mouth, his hands, the pulse in his throat, and when he wasn't she would find herself thinking about how he looked from behind, or that easy, unself-conscious way he moved that dried the breath in her throat.

Meredith had never thought of herself as a particularly sensual person before, but now all she could do was wonder what it would be like to lie next to Hal, to kiss her way along his jaw, to slip her hands beneath his shirt, to feel him smile and roll her beneath him…

She hadn't felt like this about Richard. In spite of his good looks, her attraction to Richard had been mental rather than physical, and her overwhelming sensation had been one of astonished delight at having come across a man who really was everything she'd ever wanted.

Hal most definitely *wasn't*. He could be nice, but a lot of the time he was taciturn and difficult, and he lived on the other side of the world in the kind of isolation Meredith wouldn't even have been able to imagine two weeks ago. But it was Hal who made her senses leap and sent the heat roiling through her body. He hadn't mentioned the idea of a brief affair again and Meredith told herself she was glad. It was getting harder and harder to remember how sensible she was, and just why that would have been a bad idea.

'What about you, Meredith?'

'What?' Startled out of her thoughts, Meredith almost spilt her tea.

'I've just been telling Emma and Mickey about the water hole further along the creek that's always deep enough for swimming,' said Hal. 'We thought we'd go this afternoon. Do you want to come?'

A swim sounded incredibly appealing, but Meredith thought that the less time she spent with Hal at the moment, the better it would be for her peace of mind.

'I think I should catch up with some work,' she said.

'Oh, come on, it's the weekend!'

'It'll be fun if you come too,' said Emma and Mickey nodded.

'Come on, Meredith!'

Flattered by their enthusiasm for her company, Meredith dithered. 'I haven't got a swimming costume,' she remembered, but Hal dismissed that as irrelevant.

'You don't need a cossie.'

'I'm not swimming naked!'

Hal allowed himself to picture that for a moment. 'I wasn't going to suggest that, although it's an idea…Haven't you got a T-shirt or something you could wear?'

'I wasn't expecting to be here long enough to go swimming,' Meredith pointed out. 'I haven't really got anything that casual.'

'Why don't I lend you one, then? It won't matter if you get it wet.'

'I can't keep raiding your wardrobe,' Meredith protested, aware that she had somehow been led astray from the idea of staying at home and working to the practicalities of swimming. How had that happened?

'Rubbish.' Hal pushed back his chair. 'I'll find you something when I get back. We'll all be back for lunch, but maybe you could pack some biscuits or something for afternoon smoko and we'll take it with us.'

It seemed churlish to insist on working after that and, besides, she deserved a break, Meredith decided, although she was ready to change her mind when she discovered that she was expected to ride as well as swim.

'You're not serious?' she said when Hal broke the news.

'Of course I am. You were the one who said I should give Emma and Mickey a taste of what we used to do as kids,' he said. 'That means taking the horses.'

'It would be much more sensible if we all went in the truck.'

'But would it be as much fun?' he asked, selecting a hat for her.

'It would for me. I'm a city girl, and everyone knows city girls don't ride.' Meredith decided to take a stand. 'There's no way I'm getting on a horse!' she declared, and he looked at her with one of those infuriating almost-smiles of his.

'Scared?'

'Of course I'm scared!'

'I'll put you on the oldest, slowest horse we've got,' he promised, and handed her a hat to put an end to the discussion. 'Put that on,' he said. 'I'll go and saddle up.'

Meredith had been hoping that Emma and Mickey would lobby for the truck too, but perversely they decided they liked the idea of riding and went out to help Hal catch some suitable horses, while she wrapped some flapjacks she had made that morning and wondered how she could convince them to leave her to work after all.

But Hal was having none of it. 'Come on, up you get,' he said as Meredith hung back when faced with what looked to her an enormous horse.

'I'm really not sure this is a good idea,' she prevaricated. 'What if I fall off?'

'You won't fall off. Duke here can't do more than plod and, anyway, I won't let you. Put your foot here,' he ordered, pointing at a stirrup. 'No, not that one unless you want to end up riding backwards!'

Meredith jumped around a bit while the horse stood placidly, then she felt Hal's hard hands on her, lifting her bodily into the saddle. She flopped into it, grabbing for the pommel, and hoped he would put the fiery colour in her cheeks down to exertion.

Emma and Mickey were already on two ponies, laughing at her awkwardness, and looking more animated than she had ever seen them.

True to his word, Hal set off very slowly. He had Duke on a leading rein, so that Meredith just had to concentrate on not falling off.

And on not thinking about how strong his hands had been, or how warm the brush of his fingers as he'd handed her the reins.

For the first few minutes she was too nervous to do more than clutch on and stare straight ahead, but after a while the rhythmic sway of the horse began to soothe her and she let herself relax enough to look around.

The horses were ambling through the fractured shade of the silvery-barked gums that spread out on either side of the homestead creek bed. It was hot and still and beyond the trees the light was so diamond bright that even the smallest detail seemed etched with extraordinary clarity: the peeling bark, the dried leaves carpeting the red dust, the worn leather reins in her hand.

And Hal, of course, sitting so easily on his horse beside her. He was wearing jeans, boots and a checked shirt so faded it was impossible to guess what the original colours might have been. His hat was tipped forward to shade his face and Meredith could just see the firm line of his jaw and the set of his mouth. Just looking at it gave her a hollow feeling inside and she forced her gaze forwards once more to stare instead at Duke's lazily flickering ears.

Emma and Mickey were enjoying themselves and, after a while, Meredith began to think that she might be enjoying herself as well. Being so high off the ground was alarming, but exhilarating too. When a flock of galahs took off from a tree with an explosion of sound, she watched the flash of silver to pink as they turned against the brassy blue sky and was conscious of a pang of awareness so sharp that it almost hurt.

'Do you ever think, *I'll never forget this moment*?' she asked Hal, who turned to look at her.

'I suppose this is all too familiar for me to think that,' he said, thinking about it. 'I just take it for granted. It's funny to think that it isn't normal for you.'

'No, it's not normal,' she said with a smile. 'Normal is pavements and people and traffic and buildings.'

'Are you missing London?'

'Funnily enough…I'm not,' she realised slowly.

'Well, you're not here for long. You might as well enjoy it while you're here.'

'Yes,' she agreed after a moment, but, oddly, the thought of not being there for much longer didn't seem as reassuring as it once had.

The creek bed was so dry that Meredith was beginning to think the idea of swimming was some kind of joke, but at length it fed into a much wider, deeper river whose still green waters cut so unexpectedly through the parched land that she gasped with surprise when she saw it.

'This is Whyman's Creek,' said Hal and nodded his head eastwards. 'Follow it down from here and you'll get to the town.'

'Is this where we're swimming?'

'No, it's just a little further down.'

He took them to the old water hole where he and Jack had swum so often when they had been small boys. The creek turned and dipped into some smooth red rocks at that point, and over the aeons had worn a deep green pool that stayed wet in the driest of seasons. Half hidden in the shade of gnarled old ghost gums, it was easy to miss unless you knew the way.

Hal checked his horse as it came into sight. He hadn't been here for a very long time, he realised, and the memory of Jack was suddenly, painfully vivid. He could picture his brother so clearly—scrambling fearlessly up the rocks, whooping with delight if he ever managed to beat Hal to the top—that Jack's high, boyish laugh seemed to be ringing still over the water hole.

'Can we dive off those rocks?' Mickey asked eagerly, and Hal started, brought abruptly back to the present. Clicking his teeth, he urged his horse on. Jack was gone, but there was another boy here now, other children to have fun here the way they had done.

'You can,' he told Mickey. 'That's what Jack and I used to do.'

He made himself say Jack's name deliberately, and it wasn't as hard as he'd thought it would be. 'Come on,' he said. 'Let's swim.'

He swung off his horse in one fluid movement that Meredith could only envy, while the children scrambled less elegantly off their ponies.

Humiliatingly, Meredith was forced to sit there.

'How do I get down?' she asked, and Hal came over to take the reins from her and explain what she needed to do. He held up his hands to help her down and, burningly aware of her clumsiness, Meredith ended up sliding down the hard length of his body.

Her hat fell off somewhere along the way and Hal bent to pick it up. Almost thoughtfully, he settled it back on her head. His eyes held an unfathomable expression and for one crazy moment Meredith thought that he might be about to kiss her.

But Emma and Mickey were shouting with excitement and in the end he stepped back. 'I'll tie up the horses,' was all he said.

Meredith was furious with herself. Of *course* he hadn't been going to kiss her, right there in front of the children. What a stupid idea! But her heart was hammering so loudly as she followed the sound of the children's voices on to the worn rocks surrounding the pool that she half expected them to turn and demand what all the noise was about.

They had already stripped down to their costumes. 'Can we go in now?'

Emma shrieked as she put a foot in the water. 'It's cold!'

Hal grinned. 'Didn't I tell you? You'll have to jump in.'

'You do it!'

'I'm going to.' Casually Hal tossed off his hat and pulled off his shirt before unfastening his jeans to reveal a pair of faded swimming shorts. He glanced at Meredith, who was doing her best not to stare at his body. His back was just as smooth and powerfully muscled as she had imagined.

'Aren't you coming in?'

There was no way Meredith was calmly stripping off her shirt and bra and putting on the T-shirt in front of him. It was hard enough staying upright with her heart thudding and thumping like this, let alone trying to swim. 'I'll watch for a bit,' she said and settled on a rock. It was deliciously cool in the shade and she closed her eyes for a moment, willing the pounding to subside.

'Look at Uncle Hal!'

Meredith's eyes snapped open to see Hal climbing sure-footedly up the rocks until he was standing on a ledge, high above the still surface of the pool. She was on her feet in a flash. 'Hal, that looks dangerous,' she said, her voice rising in alarm. 'I think you should come down.'

'It's fine,' he said. 'We used to dive off here all the time, Jack and I.'

And with that he dived into the pool, emerging after what seemed like a lifetime to flick the hair out of his eyes with a smile that clutched at the base of Meredith's spine.

'I'm going to do that too,' said Mickey, heading up the rocks. Emma was more hesitant, but even she had a go in the end and was thrilled with herself.

Meredith sat and watched them, torn between envy at their carefree enjoyment and disapproval of the risk involved. What if one of them slipped? What if the water wasn't as deep as they thought?

'Come on, Meredith,' they called. 'Get in here!'

The water did look wonderfully inviting. 'I'll swim,' she said, 'but I'm not jumping anywhere!'

Pulling off her shirt and bra behind the horses, Meredith slunk self-consciously back to the pool, tugging Hal's T-shirt down as far as it would go to cover her thighs. Very conscious of Hal's gaze, she dithered around by the edge of the pool, putting a toe in and then jerking it back, unprepared for quite how cold the water was.

'You know, you'd find it much easier if you just jumped in,' said Hal.

'I don't dare,' she confessed.

'Wait there,' he said.

He hauled himself, dripping, out of the pool and took Meredith's hand. His fingers were cold and wet against her hot flesh, or at least that was the reason Meredith gave herself for the fact that her heart seemed to stop as the breath evaporated from her lungs. Shock, she told herself. Nothing to do with the water droplets gleaming on his shoulders. Nothing to do with the light reflected in his grey eyes or the nearness of his taut, wet body.

'Come with me,' he said and led her over to the rocks they had climbed. Close to, they didn't seem quite as sheer and dangerous as they had from her side of the pool, but Hal still had to help her up with a mixture of pulling and encouragement, until at last Meredith stood over the pool. It probably wasn't that high, she recognised, but she was terrified.

'I can't,' she said.

'You can,' said Hal. 'Be reckless for once,' he said. 'Do something that isn't sensible. You can if you try.'

'Jump!' Emma and Mickey called from below, where they were treading water. 'It's fun!'

Fun. Didn't she deserve some of that? She spent her whole life being sensible, Meredith thought. Hal was right. Just for once, she could be reckless.

Taking a deep breath, Meredith jumped. It felt as if she were falling through the bright air in slow motion, and when the cold water closed over her head she thought her heart was going to stop with the cold, but when she broke the surface she was so exhilarated that she couldn't stop gasping and laughing.

The next moment, Hal dived in behind her. He surfaced very close, as she was still treading water, smoothing the wet hair from her face, and Meredith could swear that she could see every pore in his skin, every crease around his eyes, every single one of the dark lashes that framed them.

'Fun?' he asked her and Meredith smiled back at him, completely unaware of how lush and vivid and desirable she looked.

'Fun,' she agreed.

They splashed around with Emma and Mickey for a while, then Hal got out to make tea on the little gas burner that he had brought, tied to his saddle. He boiled some water in a battered billycan, and then tossed in some tea leaves, stirring the brew with a stick.

'Tea's up,' he called.

Meredith's exhilaration faded as she sat on a warm smooth rock and tried not to look at Hal's lean brown body. She felt pale and fat in comparison and she was embarrassed by the way Hal's T-shirt was clinging to her. It was horribly obvious that she had taken off her bra, and she pulled up her legs and clutched her mug of tea to hide as much of herself as possible.

To her relief, Hal didn't seem to be paying her much attention. He was chatting with Emma and Mickey, and every now and then Meredith judged it safe to risk a glance, only to find her eyes snagging inevitably with Hal's, who had looked over at the same moment, until the air was twanging with tension.

When Emma and Mickey wandered off to explore, Meredith watched them go in dismay. Now what was she going to do?

Be sensible, she told herself sternly, and stop being so silly. You're a grown woman and there's absolutely no reason why you can't have a normal conversation with Hal.

Apart from the fact that she was sitting here with virtually no clothes on, and the mere thought of touching him was enough to dissolve her bones and hollow her lungs.

'More tea?'

'Thanks.' Meredith cleared her throat as she held out her mug. There had been enough exhilaration this afternoon. It was time to go back to being sensible. Somehow, she had to find a way to deflect the terrible tension that was threatening to overpower her.

'It's strange to be sitting out here drinking tea when Richard's so ill,' she said.

'I thought you'd heard from Lucy that he was out of the coma?'

It was probably a good thing she had made a move to steer the conversation into safe channels, Hal reflected. She must have been aware of the simmering awareness between them, too. He had been finding it hard to cope with all week.

In spite of the fact that Meredith had vanished into the office every evening, he had been disturbingly aware of her all the time. He hadn't been able to get the feel of her out of his mind. One brief hug that was all it had been, but he could still smell her perfume, still feel the softness of her hair and the yielding warmth of her body.

Meredith was still valiantly trying to steer the conversation on to neutral ground. 'He is, but he's still very ill.'

'You're worried about him, aren't you?'

'Of course I am,' said Meredith, even though the truth was that she hadn't spent nearly as much time worrying recently. London seemed so far away out here. 'Richard is a good friend.'

'Is that all he is?'

The look Hal gave her was deeply sceptical, and she stiffened.

'What do you mean?'

Hal finished his tea and lay back on the warm rock, linking his hands behind his head. 'You seemed much more concerned about him than Lucy was,' he pointed out in a neutral voice. 'You're the one who went to all the trouble for him. Lucy went back for you, not for him.'

Meredith opened her mouth to deny it, but the words dried in her throat. There didn't seem any need to save face out here, where there was just light and space and silence. She glanced at Hal, stretched comfortably out beside her. There was a smooth rock behind her and she shifted so that she could lean against it and tip up her face to the dappled sunlight.

She told him the truth. 'I was in love with him,' she said.

CHAPTER EIGHT

'WAS? Or still are?'

'Was…I think,' said Meredith. 'I hope,' she added after a moment. She certainly didn't want to be in love with Richard.

'It's not like you not be sure,' said Hal. 'But then, I wouldn't have thought it was like you to fall in love with your sister's boyfriend either.'

Meredith rested her head against the rock. 'It wasn't like that,' she told him. 'I met Richard first, at a party, and I fell for him pretty heavily. I thought he was wonderful—charming, intelligent, attractive, interested in the same things as me…and just…*nice.*'

'Mr Perfect, in fact.' Hal couldn't quite keep the edge from his voice and he hoped Meredith didn't think it sounded as much like jealousy as it did to him.

'Yes,' she agreed. Of course, there hadn't been

that *frisson* of physical awareness with Richard, but that had only made him more perfect. She had been instantly comfortable with him. He'd never made her feel jangly and unsettled the way Hal did.

'We clicked straight away and talked all evening about France and Italy and food and music...I couldn't believe it. I'd never met anyone I liked that much who seemed to like me back, and when he suggested meeting for a drink I was over the moon. It was too good to be true.'

'So what went wrong?'

'Nothing,' said Meredith. 'We had a drink and got on just as well again, and then we arranged to go to a concert, and *that* was nice, but Richard never gave any indication that he wanted any more than to be friends.'

'And you did?' said Hal, raising his head slightly to squint up at her.

'Well, yes, I was hoping...but I don't have much confidence when it comes to men. I could understand that Richard might not find me attractive.'

Meredith pleated the bottom of the T-shirt between her fingers while Hal looked at her and wondered whether Richard had ever seen her in a damp top.

'I thought he needed more time,' she said, 'and I was terrified of spooking him by letting him know how I felt—he would have run a mile!'

'Why do you think that?'

'Because it's what any normal guy would do if faced by some woman he liked enough to have a drink with telling him that she'd decided he was perfect and that she wanted to spend the rest of her life with him and have his babies,' said Meredith dryly. 'You would have run too.'

'When you put it like that...' Hal acknowledged. 'But you didn't have to phrase it quite that way, did you? You could have just let him know that you found him attractive and wanted to take things a bit further.'

Meredith sighed. 'I was afraid to do that,' she admitted. 'I thought he would have to tell me then that he didn't want that, and then it would be too awkward for us even to be friends. So I tried to get him used to the idea. I invited him round to dinner, but told him it would be very casual, with just a couple of old friends and my sister and her boyfriend, so he wouldn't think it was a big deal.

'And he came and it was all fine,' she said,

'except Lucy was late, as usual. She arrived at last and...well, you know what Lucy's like. She lights up a room. She was laughing and saying that she had just broken it off with her boyfriend after some stupid row. They hadn't been going out for very long and it wasn't serious, but I've often wondered what would have happened if she hadn't argued with Tom that night. Because Richard took one look at Lucy and fell in love with her.

'I saw his face,' Meredith remembered. One look at him, and her heart had cracked. She had been so sure that Richard was The One. 'He looked...dazzled. It's the only word for it. And of course I'd been so careful not to tell anyone how important he was to me that I hadn't warned Lucy. She would never have flirted with him if she'd known how I felt. But she couldn't help herself. He was completely smitten and when he asked her out, she said yes.'

Hal raised himself on to one elbow and turned towards her. 'Why didn't you say anything then?'

'What would have been the point? Nothing was going to change how Richard felt once he'd seen her, and all I'd have done was make Lucy feel uncomfortable.'

'So Mr Perfect was right there, just as you'd imagined him, and Lucy walked off with him.' Hal frowned. 'How did you deal with that?'

'Well, there was no point in getting upset about it,' said Meredith briskly. 'I didn't want to lose my sister, or my friend, so I told myself that it had probably worked out for the best. At least I hadn't been tempted to make some embarrassing declaration before Richard met her.'

'And Lucy never guessed?'

'Not immediately. But she came round about a month later, and it was obvious that she was getting bored. Richard was too adoring, I think. Lucy needs someone who's a bit more of a challenge. Anyway,' Meredith went on, smoothing out the wrinkles in the T-shirt, 'she was talking about him and…I don't know how I betrayed myself, but there must have been something in my expression because she suddenly stopped and stared at me, and she *knew*.'

'It must have been difficult for her too, when she realised,' Hal commented.

'She was furious with me for not telling her. And then, being Lucy, she went off and told Richard she was going to Australia in some big, melodramatic gesture because she felt so bad about what she'd done!'

Meredith sighed. 'It didn't really help. Richard was devastated, and he'd come round all the time and want to sit and talk about Lucy and why she had suddenly gone. Of course, I couldn't tell him it was because of me. I felt awful for him. He really loved Lucy and he didn't deserve to lose her like that. I'd accepted it by then anyway,' she said. 'I just wanted him to be happy, and he wasn't.'

'So when he had that accident, you tried to make everything right for him.'

'What's wrong with that?' she asked defensively.

'It doesn't work like that,' said Hal. 'You spend too much time trying to make everyone else's life better, Meredith. You decide what they need and you make it happen, but they have to work it out for themselves.'

'It's better than not doing anything to help, surely?'

'But you're so busy looking after everyone else, you're not living your own life properly.'

With a gasp of outrage, Meredith sat bolt upright. 'How can you *say* that?' she demanded furiously. 'I've got a great life, thank you very much! I've got my own house, lots of friends, a successful career…'

'Maybe you have,' said Hal calmly, 'but you're too scared to take a risk where it matters.'

'Oh, yes?' Her voice dripped scorn. 'Like what?'

'Like telling Richard how you felt,' he said. 'It would have saved everyone a lot of trouble if you had just been honest about what you wanted. Maybe Richard *didn't* want you as more than a friend, but you never gave yourself the chance to find out if he did. Maybe he thought you weren't interested in *him*.'

'Now you sound like Lucy!' said Meredith sulkily, sinking back against her rock.

'Lucy's a lot smarter than she looks.' Hal's glance was pointed. 'At least she's not afraid of life.'

'I'm not *afraid*!'

'Yes, you are,' he said. 'You're always sensible, always careful, always worrying about what might go wrong if you reached out for what you wanted. You don't have to be like that, Meredith,' he went on more gently. 'You could be like you were just now, when you jumped off that rock. You wanted to do it and you did, and it felt good, didn't it?'

'Yes,' she admitted, 'but life's not just about jumping off rocks. You can't always have what you want.'

Hal pulled himself up into a sitting position and turned to face her. 'The trouble is, Meredith, you might never get what you want if you're too afraid to ask for it.'

'Oh, and I suppose you do?' she said in a bolshie voice, not enjoying the way this conversation was going.

'I know what I want, yes,' he said. 'Right now, I want you.'

There was a reverberating silence while his words seemed to ring around the water hole, bouncing off the rocks and echoing out into the vastness of the outback. *I want you...want you...want you.*

Meredith swallowed hard. 'Because I'm convenient?' she managed at last.

'No,' said Hal. 'Because I think you're beautiful and sexy and brave and true.'

Nobody had ever said anything like that to Meredith before, and for a long, long moment she could just stare at him, the breath clogging in her throat. She didn't know what to say. She longed to believe him, but how could she? She had never been beautiful, never been sexy. She was brisk and bossy and sensible.

Ah, yes, remember sensible?

'You don't want me for ever, though,' she pointed out.

'No,' Hal agreed. 'You know how I feel about commitment. Forevers don't last. You're too much of a city girl ever to stay in a place like Wirrindago, even if you wanted to. I know you'll go back to London sooner or later, probably sooner, but that doesn't mean I don't want you very much while you're here.'

He paused, his eyes on Meredith's face. 'The question is, are you brave enough to admit that you want me too? Will you let yourself enjoy some fun and some excitement while it lasts? You never know, it might feel as good as jumping off that rock!'

Meredith looked away at the water. She was tempted—of course she was—and it was no use pretending that she didn't want him. But...

'Why don't you take a risk for once, Meredith?' Hal's voice was deep and low, and it sent tiny shivers over her skin. How could he do that when he wasn't even touching her? 'Or are you really that afraid?'

'It's not that,' she said at last. Her mouth was dry and she was desperately hanging on to the shreds of self-control. In the distance, she could hear Emma and Mickey's voices echoing over the rocks and she remembered at last one good reason to be sensible.

'It's not that I don't want to,' she admitted at last. 'I just...don't think it would be appropriate while the children are here.'

There was a pause and then Hal smiled, accepting defeat. 'Well, at least "not appropriate" is a better reason to say no than "not sensible",' he said. 'And you've got a point,' he conceded as he hoisted himself to his feet and looked down at Meredith, still sitting against her rock. She was looking up at him, violet eyes wide and dark with what he hoped was temptation. 'But if you ever change your mind, Meredith, all you have to do is let me know.'

Hal's words echoed constantly in her mind over the next few days. *Change your mind...change your mind...* The truth was that Meredith thought about changing it all the time, and no matter how often she reminded herself about Emma and Mickey, there was always that deep, dark tug of desire, that insidious voice whispering *why not?* and reminding her of that glorious exhilaration as she'd plunged into that cold water and surfaced into the glittering sunlight. She wanted to feel that good again, didn't she?

Meredith tried throwing herself into her work, but it was hard to concentrate. She would look out of the window and there would be Hal, crossing the yard with that loose, rangy stride, stopping to talk to the dog in the shade. Watching him bend down was enough to make the longing surge dizzyingly through her and when she forced her eyes back to the computer, the words on the screen blurred in front of her eyes.

So when a big car pulled up in the yard, Meredith was delighted at the distraction. A visitor was just what she needed.

A woman about her own age climbed down from the car and stretched. She smiled when she saw Meredith appear on the veranda. 'Hi,' she said. 'I'm Lydia. I've come to take Emma and Mickey home.'

'We weren't expecting you back for a while,' Meredith admitted as they went into the homestead. 'Hal expected to have them for a couple of months.'

'I know, that's what we planned but…well, when Greg and I got there, we realised how much we missed the kids and wished that we had them with us. We decided that we'd made a mistake. We did need time alone together, but we needed to be a family together more, so I've come back to collect Emma and Mickey and Greg is cutting short his trip and is going to fly back to Sydney as soon as he can.'

Emma and Mickey had been out with Hal to check the salt licks and were delighted to see their mother when they all came in together, but were typically now reluctant to leave. Since the day at the water hole, they had been spending more time with their uncle and had now quite forgotten how bored and homesick they had been at first.

'Do we *have* to?' they asked when Lydia told them they were going home, probably exactly as they had said it when she had told them about going to Wirrindago. 'Can't we stay a bit longer?'

'Only a couple of days,' warned Lydia. 'We've

got to return the car to Townsville, and then we're going back to Sydney. Dad's flying back early so we can all be together.'

Meredith was envious of their closeness as a family. Although the children moaned, they obviously loved their mother and were excited at the thought of seeing their father again. She liked Lydia, who was more open than Hal and obviously loved Wirrindago while being realistic about the fact that she could never live there again.

'Greg's a businessman,' she said, 'and we have a good life in Sydney, but I will have to try and bring the kids back here more often. They've obviously loved it.'

Lydia helped Meredith to get lunch the next day. 'I wish Hal would have kids,' she said, washing the lettuce she had brought with her as a treat from Townsville. 'It would be so good for him to have a family of his own.'

She glanced under her lashes at Meredith, who was annoyed to find herself flushing. 'I gathered he didn't want to get married,' she said carefully.

'Oh, that's what he *says*, but it's nonsense,' said Lydia, dismissive as only a sister could be. 'He needs a wife.'

'I guess it's not that easy to find someone suitable out here,' said Meredith, trying to sound non-committal. 'There aren't that many opportunities to meet people.'

'There's you,' Lydia pointed out slyly.

'There's nothing between me and Hal,' Meredith said, firmly cutting the bread.

'Isn't there? I've seen the way you look at each other, especially when you think the other one isn't looking. I don't quite know what it is, but it certainly isn't nothing!'

'No, honestly,' she insisted. 'I'm just standing in for my sister. Didn't Hal tell you? I don't belong here.'

'Funny,' said Lydia, 'you seem to me to belong perfectly.'

Meredith looked up from the loaf, astounded. 'Me? But I'm a city girl!'

'Really?' Lydia smiled as if humouring her. 'You seem to have adapted very well then.'

And it was true, Meredith thought. She was getting used to the outback in a way she would never have dreamed possible when she'd first arrived. It was ridiculous to say that she belonged, but, yes, she was learning to appreciate the stillness and the silence and the dazzling light.

Just in time to go back to the greyness and the dampness and the crowds of London.

Meredith returned to cutting the bread. 'I'm leaving soon,' she told Lydia. 'Just as soon as my sister comes back.'

'Shame,' said Lydia lightly. 'Well, I'll just have to find someone else for Hal. He's been on his own too long.' She started slicing tomatoes. 'The trouble is that he's never got over the way our mother left.'

'He told me,' said Meredith and Lydia looked at her in surprise. '*Did* he? He doesn't normally talk about it. Did he tell you about Jack too?'

Meredith nodded and Lydia's gaze rested on her thoughtfully.

'It was worse for Hal,' she said. 'To be honest, I don't remember much about that time, but Hal was older. He remembers everything, and I think he feels responsible, as if he should have somehow known what Jack was going to do. Dad was broken up and it was Hal who had to hold everything together until our aunt arrived.'

'It must have been hard for him,' said Meredith. 'For all of you.'

Lydia shrugged practically. 'We did all right. And you have to move on. It's such a pity Hal's engagement to Jill didn't work out. It made him think that no woman would ever stick it at Wirrindago, and that if he did get married, history would repeat itself, but lots of people have very happy marriages out here, and you can have unhappy marriages in a city. It's nothing to do with the place.'

'Still, you'd have to love somebody a lot to be prepared to live somewhere like Wirrindago all the time,' said Meredith.

'Yes,' said Lydia, looking at her seriously. 'You would.'

Meredith was sad to see them go the next day. 'It's going to be quiet without you,' she told Emma and Mickey as she hugged them goodbye.

'I wish we could stay,' said Emma, clinging to her.

'Now, don't start that again,' said Lydia briskly. 'You know you're looking forward to getting home and seeing Dad and it's not as if it's goodbye for ever. We'll come out and see Uncle Hal again next year.'

'And you,' said Emma loyally to Meredith, who found that her throat was suddenly tight.

'No, I won't be here,' she said, but she couldn't imagine not being there. She couldn't imagine being back in her London house, with no galahs screeching in the trees, no fierce blue sky, no red earth.

No Hal.

But she couldn't imagine staying here for ever either. She would go nuts with boredom. OK, she hadn't had time to be bored yet, but if she was here all the time…of course she would get bored.

Wouldn't she?

Not that there was any question of staying for ever. Even if Lucy hadn't been coming back, Hal had made it clear that any relationship would be a strictly temporary one, so getting involved would be pointless.

Wouldn't it?

Completely pointless, Meredith told herself, but she was very aware of Hal standing next to her as they waved off Lydia and the children. When the car had disappeared and the dust had settled, they still hadn't moved. They weren't even looking at each other, but the air around them was so taut that Meredith had to suck in extra oxygen. Funny to be standing out here with hundreds of miles of space around them and to feel that there wasn't enough air to breathe.

'Well,' she said, as the silence threatened to smother them.

'Well,' said Hal.

He turned and looked at her for a moment. Her hair had grown out into a softer style since she'd arrived. It was curling now around her face, the sun picking up gold at its tips, and she had a hand to her forehead to shade her face. She was wearing the old shirt that he had given her for cooking, and she looked warm and alluring and somehow *right* standing there beside him.

I won't be here, she had told Emma.

Hal tried to imagine how it would be when she had gone, when he wouldn't be able to walk inside and find her in the kitchen, or hard at work in the study, or quiet and still on the veranda at night, but his mind shied away from the image of emptiness and loneliness.

Which was ridiculous. He'd never been lonely before, and he certainly wasn't about to start now.

'We'll be back for lunch,' he said gruffly and strode off.

Meredith watched him go and felt the familiar

roil of desire in her entrails before she made herself go back inside. And be sensible.

But, no matter how hard she concentrated on all the reasons why it would be stupid—more than stupid, *ridiculous*—to get involved, Meredith couldn't stop her heart crashing into her throat when she heard Hal's boots on the wooden steps at lunch time. All the men came in for lunch, but she was only aware of him. She felt as if her whole body was charged with electricity, and kept waiting for him to stare at her and ask her why she was buzzing and humming.

He wasn't handsome. He wasn't Richard. He wasn't perfect. But she wanted to touch him more than she could ever remember wanting anything before. She wanted to be able to go round to the end of the table, to put her arms around him from behind and bend down to kiss the side of his neck. She wanted to run her hands over his back, under his shirt, to whisper that she didn't care if they both had work to do and that it was the middle of the day, she just wanted him to take her to bed…

Meredith swallowed hard and wondered if she was actually running a fever. That would account for the heat that kept washing through her, the light-headedness, the churning in her stomach, the way her bones had turned to liquid. She needed to lie down.

Or she needed to sort herself out.

Think of it as a fever, she told herself. It just needs to work its way through your system. And you can help it on its way. All you have to do is tell Hal that you've changed your mind.

The more Meredith thought about it, the more she thought that was exactly what she needed to do. Why was she even hesitating? She was twenty-eight, for heaven's sake, and she had never had a passionate physical affair. At this rate, she was never going to have *any* kind of affair, and she would dwindle into a sensible, practical middle age knowing that she had never been wild or reckless or simply taken what had been offered.

It wasn't a big deal. It wasn't going to last with Hal—they both knew that—but surely that made it even better? Meredith persuaded herself. Neither of them would have any false expectations. It would just be…a physical thing.

At the thought of just how physical it might be,

a shiver of pure desire snaked down Meredith's spine. She was supposed to be working but the words on the screen kept blurring as she pictured Hal instead, settling his hat on his head, the way the stern mouth relaxed into a smile, the unself-conscious grace with which he swung himself into the saddle. And she remembered his face as he had turned to her and said that he wanted her—the creases around those strangely light eyes, the planes of his face, the line of his mouth, the faint stubble on his jaw—and the mere memory was enough to turn her entrails into a churning, molten mass.

She could do it. Meredith was half scared by her own daring, by acting so out of character. All she had to do was say it, and she could give in to this longing to press her lips to his throat, to kiss her way along his jaw, to taste his mouth and feel his body, lean and hard beneath her hands...

If you ever change your mind, Meredith, all you have to do is let me know.

There was something about the light here, something about the space that made her want to cast off the shackles that usually held her, made her want to do something different, *be* different.

She was sick of being sensible, sick of thinking about the long term. She wanted to be rash and impulsive. She wanted to follow her heart instead of her head for once.

Maybe it would be a mistake. Maybe it would be humiliating. Maybe she would be hurt, but she didn't care. She was going to try.

If she could find the words.

By the time supper ended, Meredith was so jittery and jangly with nerves that she couldn't eat—and that was a first!

'Not hungry?' asked Hal as she pushed her plate aside.

Her eyes, which had been skittering around looking everywhere except at him, met his, and her heart lurched. 'No,' she said huskily.

It seemed an age before the stockmen got up to go. They had all wanted second helpings of the apple pie she had made, which would have been flattering if she hadn't wanted to scream at them to eat up and *go away*!

But at last they were gone. Meredith's pulse was booming and thumping so loudly that she could hardly hear the clink of dishes as she gathered them up.

'I'll do this,' said Hal. 'Why don't you have a night off? Go and sit on the veranda and I'll bring you some coffee.'

Meredith didn't want any coffee, but she thought it might be a chance to compose herself and think about what she was going to say. And there was no doubt it would be easier in the dark than in the harsh fluorescent light of the kitchen.

I want you? Too bald.

Kiss me? Too presumptuous.

*I've been thinking and…*oh, God, no, she would dither on for hours if she started on that track.

She still hadn't decided by the time Hal came out, kicking open the screen door as he had a mug in each hand.

'It's quiet without the kids,' he said as he sat down in the chair next to hers.

'Yes, the house feels a bit empty.' She swallowed. 'It's just us now.'

'Just us,' Hal agreed.

In the dim light, Meredith could see his fingers curled around the mug and she let her eyes drift up his shirt to where it was open at the neck. She had left her own mug untouched, knowing that her hands were trembling too much to hold it properly, and her fingers tingled with the need to reach out and touch him, to lay her hand on his thigh, perhaps, or on his wrist where his sleeve was rolled casually back to reveal strong forearms with fine dark hairs. She knew suddenly that if she didn't say something right now, she was going to explode.

'Do you remember that day at the water hole?'

He turned to look at her, that almost-smile denting the corner of his mouth. 'When I told you I wanted you?'

'Yes,' she said, the breath leaking out of her.

'You said that it wouldn't be appropriate for us to sleep together when Emma and Mickey were around,' Hal reminded her, and then paused. 'Emma and Mickey aren't around any more,' he pointed out softly.

'No.' Meredith's throat was so dry that she could hardly speak, and the word came out as little more than a croak. 'No.'

Hal put down his coffee very carefully. 'Do you still think it's a bad idea?'

'Probably,' said Meredith. 'It's probably not very sensible, but I don't want to be sensible. I've had enough of being sensible.'

'Good.' A real smile curled Hal's mouth at last. 'So what do you want, Meredith?'

'I want you,' she said, as baldly as he had said it at the water hole. 'Not for ever,' she added quickly before he could object. 'Just for now.'

His smile deepened. 'Sounds good to me.'

There was a pause while they looked at each other. Meredith hadn't thought this far. She had assumed that once she'd got the message across that she'd changed her mind, Hal would take over.

'So,' she said nervously.

'So,' said Hal. 'What do you want to do with me?'

'Do with you?' she echoed with a blank look.

'You said you wanted me, and I'm all yours. Stop being careful and sensible, Meredith. Do what *you* want for once.'

So Meredith got up and made to slide on to his lap, only to hesitate at the last moment. 'I'll be too heavy for you,' she worried.

'No, you won't...come here.' Hal pulled her down so that she fell against him, but he dropped his hands almost immediately to show that she was in control.

'That's better,' he said. 'Now, do what you like!'

It felt scarily wonderful and thrilling and curiously right to be so close to him. Meredith stopped worrying about whether he had pins and needles in his leg from her weight. She stopped thinking about anything other than the fact that he was there, and she could do what she had been dreaming about for so long.

So she pressed her mouth to his throat, where she had watched the pulse beating below his ear, then slowly, slowly, she kissed her way along his jaw, revelling in the feel of his rough skin beneath her lips, tantalising, taking her time...

'Is it OK if I do this?' she whispered.

'It's very OK.' Hal's voice was ragged with the effort of self-control as Meredith kissed her way onwards, a blizzard of light kisses, until she reached his mouth. She could feel its corner curling into a smile and she smiled back, her lips on his.

At last—at last!—his hands came up to secure her against him, putting an end to the teasing as they kissed—a long, deep, hungry kiss that went on and on until Meredith thought that she would shatter with the sheer pleasure of it.

She sank into the rush of warmth and sweetness, into the absolute certainty that her lips had been *made* to kiss his mouth. It was slightly worrying, that, she thought hazily. It shouldn't feel this good, shouldn't feel this *right*, but the brief tug of practicality was swamped beneath a gathering excitement as his hand slid up her thigh, warm and insistent, rucking up her skirt.

'You don't know how much I've wanted to do this,' he murmured. 'Every time you put on one of your skirts, I wanted to do this.'

'I thought my skirts were impractical?' she said, breathless beneath the wickedly pleasurable onslaught of his hands and his mouth.

'Not for this,' said Hal, and they laughed shakily before they were both submerged in the swirl of spinning, shivery sensation.

Meredith's fingers were fumbling at the buttons of his shirt when Hal tipped her off his lap and stood up without losing hold of her hand. 'I think it's time we moved somewhere more comfortable, don't you?'

Her head cleared slightly as he took her down to his room, so much so that she hung back at the door, suddenly losing her nerve. Was she really doing the right thing?

'You're not turning sensible on me, are you, Meredith?'

Meredith looked at him and she had a sudden image of herself leaping off the rock, of the sheer joy of that moment. 'No,' she said, and she smiled as he drew her into his bedroom and closed the door. 'I don't feel like being sensible now.'

CHAPTER NINE

'How does it feel?' Hal asked, much, much later when they were lying entangled with the sheet, his hand smoothing lazily over the dips and curves of her body.

Meredith smiled. She felt utterly replete and relaxed. It didn't matter that she wasn't the slender beauty she had always longed to be. She wasn't dumpy and plain any more. Hal had made her feel beautiful and desirable, and she was glowing with the knowledge of her own gorgeousness.

She turned on her side to run her own hand over his lean flank. 'It feels wonderful,' she said.

'I meant not being sensible,' he said with mock severity.

'That too.'

That leap into the bright air above the water hole had been nothing compared to the tumbling, glittery rush of making love, of Hal's lips on her skin, of the sureness of his hands, of the taste of him and the hard possession of his body.

They had been sensible enough to take some precautions, Meredith remembered, but otherwise, no, she hadn't been at all sensible and it had been glorious.

'I think I could get used to not being sensible,' she said, stretching luxuriously and looking around her for the first time.

Hal's room was as plain and masculine as she would have expected, with little furniture apart from the bed, a chair and a solid chest of drawers. Tucked into the mirror that sat on top of it was the photograph Meredith had found. She was glad to see that he had kept it, but it was a timely reminder too of just how determined Hal was to avoid anything more than a temporary relationship.

'Never,' Hal was saying. 'I know you. You'll be back to practical, sensible Meredith soon. Aha!' he said, seeing the flicker in her eyes and smoothing the hair tenderly away from her face. 'I can tell you've had a sensible thought already! Come on, out with it!'

Meredith would have loved to have denied it,

but she couldn't. 'I was just thinking that I *mustn't* get too used to it,' she admitted. 'Tonight was so lovely, but it's not going to last for ever, is it? Lucy will be coming back soon.'

Hal's drifting hands stilled. 'Has she said so?'

'No, her messages are all a bit vague, but she *has* said Richard is getting better.' There was a tiny crease of concern between Meredith's brows. 'I don't know what's going on. Every time I hear from her I expect her to tell me that she's getting the next plane back. She was so desperate to come back to Kevin, but she hasn't mentioned him so much recently, and he's stopped asking about her. Have you noticed?'

'Kevin isn't that chatty,' Hal pointed out, resuming his delicious exploration.

His hand moving possessively over her made Meredith arch with pleasure, but she couldn't quite push her concern about Lucy from her mind. 'Do you think I should tell her that he doesn't seem to be missing her that much and suggest that she comes back as soon as she can?'

'No, I don't,' said Hal firmly. 'I don't think you should tell anybody anything. Lucy can sort out her own life,' he told her.

'But what if she doesn't come back?' Meredith voiced the thought that had been nagging her at last. 'What then?'

There was a pause. 'Then…I guess you'd want to go home,' he said after a moment.

'Of course I would,' said Meredith a little too quickly.

And she *would*, she reminded herself. She had a house, friends, a career. Of course she would want to go back to them all.

She couldn't help wondering what she would have said if Hal had asked her to stay, but caught herself up almost immediately. There was no point in wondering. He would never have asked her that. Not once had he ever talked about the possibility of her staying. Hal didn't want anyone to stay, remember?

And, even if he did, she certainly wasn't going to give up her life in London for an outback man with major commitment issues, no matter how heart-shaking a lover he was.

That really *wouldn't* be sensible.

'I don't think you need to worry about that anyway,' said Hal. 'Lucy was pretty adamant she wanted to come back.'

'That's true.' Meredith tried to feel more relieved at the prospect of Lucy's return.

'So you'll be able to go home when she does,' he went on, forcing himself to remember all the reasons why it would be better if she did. He wasn't going to tie himself down to anyone, let alone a city girl. And certainly not a city girl whose idea of the perfect man was one who hadn't even had the sense to realise that beneath that brisk exterior lay a creature so sweet and passionate that the breath had stopped in his throat.

No, Meredith would be leaving, and he wouldn't forget it. But he was allowed to hope that it wouldn't be too soon, wasn't he?

He rolled her beneath him, savouring the feel of her. She was every bit as warm and as soft and spirited as he had imagined. 'And in the meantime…'

'In the meantime?' Meredith prompted, smiling as she twined her arms around his neck and brought his head down for a lingering kiss.

'In the meantime…there's just you and me and a few weeks to enjoy each other.'

'Then let's do that,' she whispered against his mouth. 'It's not for long. Let's make the most of it.'

Of course, keeping the temporary nature of their relationship in mind was a lot easier said than done. *A few weeks...not for long...* Periodically, Meredith would remind herself of the reality, but it was all too easy to forget.

She had never felt so uninhibited, so unfettered, so *selfish*. It was only now that she realised how much time she'd spent fretting about other people—usually Lucy and recently Richard—but other friends too. Hal had been right, Meredith realised. There was no reason for her to feel responsible for everyone else's happiness.

It was a strange feeling to think now only about her own. Meredith had never felt so at home in her body, had never felt so desired, so relaxed.

So happy.

The pattern of her days didn't change. She still got up in the darkness of the early morning to make breakfast. Now that Emma and Mickey had gone, she had more time to work, but there was still smoko and lunch and supper to prepare, still dust to be swept from the verandas. The chooks still had to be fed and clients had to be emailed and translations had to be done.

But, after supper, there was Hal. Meredith was in thrall to his touch and to the long nights of honeyed sweetness when it seemed impossible that this time would ever end. Every now and then, she would tell herself that she really ought to be sensible and think about the future, but the future meant saying goodbye to Hal, never holding him again, never touching him again, and she didn't want to think about it. She had now, and while they lay together and talked and laughed and made love and felt complete, that was enough.

'We're mustering in near the paddocks tomorrow,' said Hal one night as they cleared up after supper. 'It'll mean an early start.'

'How early?' asked Meredith, who was having trouble wrenching herself away from him in the mornings as it was.

'We'll need breakfast at four thirty.'

'I'll have to go to bed now if I need to get up

at four o'clock,' she grumbled, but she didn't really mind.

Meredith loved being part of station life and she was thrilled when Hal suggested the next morning that she meet them on the muster. She had heard about the way they rounded up the cattle from a wide area and herded them back to the yards and she was longing to see it for herself. Hal had explained that if the paddocks were open enough they would use helicopter contractors to help push the cattle in the right direction, but that day's muster began in rocky country and they would be doing it the old-fashioned way, on horseback.

'Can you drive?' he asked her.

'Of course.' Meredith wasn't sure if she was disappointed or relieved to discover that she wasn't supposed to get herself there on horseback.

'Do you think you could bring smoko out when you meet us? We'll need a break by then and I don't particularly want to take anything with us.'

'How will I find you?' she asked a little doubtfully.

Hal drew an imaginary map on the kitchen table with his finger. 'Go through the third gate on the track and then follow the fence till you come to the creek. You'll be able to get across at this time of year, then just keep going until you meet us.'

'What if I miss you? Those are big paddocks!'

'Just look for a lot of cattle,' said Hal. 'We'll be there.'

Meredith smiled to herself as she drove the truck over the bumpy paddock later that morning. She was thinking about the night before and the night to come, and enjoying the light and the huge sky above her. Funny to remember how oppressive she had found all the space at first. Then, she had felt small, crushed by the size of everything. Now, instead of feeling dwarfed, she felt taller, much taller and more complete than she had been when she'd arrived.

Hal had taken her out riding several times and, while she didn't think she would ever master the art of getting on and off a horse gracefully, Meredith had enjoyed it far more than she had expected. Hal's eyes were always moving and he had taught her to count any cattle that she saw, to note where they were and what they were doing and what kind of condition they were in.

Now she cast a knowledgeable eye over two cows that stood by the fence, their floppy ears flickering the flies away, eyeing her incuriously as she closed the gate behind her and got back into the truck. Shorthorns crossed with Brahmins, she decided, not like the fat cattle at home, but their coats had a lovely sheen to them. Hal would be pleased.

Then she laughed at herself. Who would have thought that the ultimate city girl would ever have found herself looking at *cows* with interest? That she would actually enjoy bumping slowly over a dried creek bed and thinking that the ghost gums were beautiful? Well, it was just part of this time out of time, Meredith reassured herself. It was like a holiday, where she could pretend to be someone completely different, someone joyous and open and not sensible at all.

Someone else, not her.

As Hal had promised, it was impossible to miss them. At first, all Meredith could see was a great cloud of dust churned up by thousands of hooves drifting in the distance. She had never seen so many cattle together at one time, she thought, driving very carefully through the leaders who had blundered to a halt as they realised that the whooping and chivvying that had kept them moving all morning had stopped. The dust was slowly settling and the cattle had started to graze or simply stand, grateful for the rest.

Kevin had spotted her in the truck and came riding over to point towards a clearing, where some of the other men had already dismounted. Slouched in his saddle in his hat and checked shirt, he looked so much the archetypal cowboy that Meredith could suddenly see why Lucy had fallen for him. Kevin might be tongue-tied at the table, but out here he was in his element.

It was clearly a favourite stopping place, for there were several fallen trees, worn smooth with use, arranged around a cleared area where once they had obviously built a careful fire to boil up tea. Fire was a terrible risk, though, and Meredith had a gas burner with her this time. She took it out of the trunk along with a big, battered billy that Kevin filled from the big water carrier.

'Where's Hal?' she asked as one of the stockmen lit the gas expertly and settled the billy to boil on top.

'He was at the back, bringing along the stragglers,' said Kevin. His eyes narrowed, recognising the familiar figure appearing through the dust haze. He pointed behind Meredith.

'There he is.'

Meredith had a sudden sharp memory of Bill, the publican in Whyman's Creek, pointing at Hal behind her shoulder and saying, 'That's the man you want'. She turned, as she had turned then, and saw Hal.

This time, he wasn't in a bad mood. He was pulling up a big snorting horse, and it seemed to Meredith that his smile was just for her, and when he swung off his horse and walked towards her it was as if she had taken an unwary step and tripped over the edge of a cliff. She could feel herself falling, falling, tumbling uncontrollably into the reality she hadn't wanted to face.

So that was why they called it falling in love, she thought with a strange, detached part of her mind. It was an extraordinarily physical sensation—the lurch of the stomach, the catch of the breath, the clutch at the heart and that strange, dizzying sensation, like a kind of vertigo, pulling her down by some irresistible force. And at the end, smashing into the truth so hard that there was no way you could pretend it wasn't there any more.

She was in love with Hal.

It wasn't just chemistry, it wasn't just sex. It was this man—*this* one—Hal and only Hal. He wasn't perfect, he wasn't even nearly perfect, but he was the one. Meredith felt very odd. It didn't make sense, but at the same time it was so blindingly obvious that she couldn't believe that she hadn't realised before.

She must have replied to Hal, but later she couldn't remember what she had said. She knew that she had made tea. She had poured it out into battered enamel mugs and handed around a tin of rock cakes she had made, but it was almost as if an impostor called Meredith who looked like her and sounded like her was going through the motions.

The real Meredith couldn't think of anything but how she was going to deal with this new knowledge. It made her feel strangely clumsy, as if she had acquired an extra limb that was throwing her off balance. How could she have let this happen? She wasn't supposed to fall in love with Hal. That hadn't been the plan.

Meredith wanted to deny it, but she couldn't. She wanted to pretend that it wasn't there at all, but she couldn't. She wanted to tell Hal, but she couldn't do that either. That was the last thing she could do. And what would have been the point?

He could hardly have been more clear about what he wanted, after all. No commitment, no talk of forever, no love. Just for now, he had said, and she had agreed. It would be a temporary thing, fun while it lasted, but they both knew that it would never be any more than that.

It wasn't Hal's fault that she had fallen in love with him, and she wouldn't embarrass him by telling him either. It would only make things awkward when the time came to go, as come it would. Even if by some chance Lucy changed her mind, she wouldn't be able to stay for ever. Hal didn't want her. Her visa would run out. She would have no choice but to go home.

She was going to have to find a way to say goodbye without Hal guessing how she felt, Meredith realised. She was going to have to find a way of convincing *herself* that it was what she needed to do, and really that shouldn't be hard. If there was no future with Hal, the sooner she left and got on with the rest of her life, the better.

'Is something wrong?' Hal asked that night as Meredith lay close but quiet beside him.

'No,' said Meredith. 'Nothing's wrong.'

'You seem a bit…withdrawn.'

'I was just thinking about home,' she said.

It was true. She had been thinking about how it would feel to be back in her own house, with no screen door, no raucous galahs, no silent creek in the distance, no Hal. She had been wondering how she was going to bear it.

'Ah,' said Hal. 'Is there news of Richard?'

'Nothing new. He's sitting up in bed now and he can have a proper conversation.'

'It sounds as if he's getting better, then.'

Hal tried his best to sound encouraging, but he suspected he didn't do it very well. Ever since Meredith had told him how perfect she had thought Richard was, he had found the idea of the other man vaguely irritating.

No, *deeply* irritating.

'You must be pleased,' he said, trying to smooth the jealousy from his voice.

'Yes, yes, of course I am.' Meredith took a breath. 'You should be pleased too,' she said. 'Once Richard's better, Lucy will be coming back. You should have your cook back soon.'

There was a tiny silence. 'I'll miss your

pastry,' said Hal after a moment, deliberately keeping it casual. 'Can you teach Lucy to make it before you go? Her pies aren't nearly as good as yours.'

Meredith's jaw ached with the effort of smiling. 'I'll leave her the recipe,' she said.

After a moment, Hal took her hand and entwined his fingers with hers. 'Your pastry isn't all I'm going to miss,' he said quietly, and she made herself smile again as she let him pull her close.

'I know,' she whispered into his throat.

It was true, Meredith thought the next morning as she picked lemons for a drizzle cake she planned to make later. He *would* miss her. She believed him about that. They had had a wonderful time together.

But he wouldn't miss her enough to ask her to stay. He wouldn't take that risk. His mother's abandonment had scarred him too deeply.

Whenever Meredith thought of what his mother had done to her children, she wanted to weep. Hal deserved the happiness of a family of his own. He deserved to be loved, even if it wasn't by her. He might have been gruff with

Emma and Mickey, but he had looked after them, had played in the water hole and taken them riding. They would have felt safe with him. You'd always feel safe when you were with Hal. When he held you, you felt he'd never let you go.

But he would let her go.

Meredith jerked another lemon free, then stopped in surprise as she heard the phone ring in the office. There were rarely any calls at this time. Most people who wanted to get in touch knew that Hal was out most of the day and tended to ring at mealtimes. She had better get it in case it was important.

But, as she turned to run for the veranda, the ringing stopped. Hal must still be there, she thought with relief. He had come back from the yards a little earlier saying something about road trains and agisment as he'd headed into the office and Meredith had just nodded, understanding that he was going to make some calls but nothing more than that.

Slowly, she made her way back to the lemon tree. It was such a treat to pick your own lemons. She wouldn't be able to do that in London.

There were a lot of things she wouldn't be able to do in London, Meredith realised sadly. She wouldn't be able to watch Hal walk across the yard with a thrill of possession, knowing that when everyone else had gone he would be all hers. She wouldn't be able to slide her hands over him and kiss her way down the long, lean body. She wouldn't be able to sleep curled into his solid back and wake with the safe weight of his arm across her.

Inside the office, Hal held the phone to his ear and watched Meredith reach up for a lemon. She pulled it from the tree, then held it to her nose to breathe in its freshness and its scent. She was wearing his old shirt, and the thought of the lush body beneath the soft material made his body tighten.

It was hard to remember now how brisk and unappealing she had seemed at first, before he knew her sweetness and her warmth and her strength. She moved more slowly now and she had a glow, a bloom, that hadn't been there before. She didn't look like a city girl any more. She looked as if she belonged here.

God, he was going to miss her.

With an effort, he dragged his attention back to the phone call.

'So you see,' Lucy was saying, 'it's really important that Meredith comes home as soon as possible.' She hesitated. 'Has she told you how she feels about Richard?'

'A bit,' said Hal.

'She probably told you that she's not in love with him any more,' said Lucy. 'She insists that she's over it, but Meredith isn't the kind of person who loves easily, and if she *does* love you, she doesn't just stop. She's just not like that. I know she comes across as a bit brisk sometimes, but underneath she's the warmest and kindest person you could ever hope to meet.'

Hal looked at Meredith through the window. He didn't need Lucy to tell him that. 'I know,' he said.

'The thing is, I think Richard's perfect for her and he's been talking about her so much... Well, I'm sure that if she came home now she'd find that everything had changed. He keeps saying how much he misses talking to her.'

He would miss talking to her, Hal wanted to shout, and it hadn't taken an accident to make him appreciate Meredith.

'I know this might cause problems for you, Hal,' Lucy was saying. 'I'm really sorry to let you down.' She hesitated. 'It's all a bit complicated, but…well, I don't think I'll be coming back after all. But if I tell Meredith that, she'll insist on staying until you've found someone else and I really think she should come home now. I owe this to her. She's the best person in the world and she deserves to be happy.'

'Yes,' said Hal slowly. 'She does.'

Lucy seemed so determined to prove to him how perfect Richard was for Meredith and how Meredith would have her heart's desire if only Hal would let her go, that in the end Hal could stand it no longer.

'I'll get Meredith for you, Lucy,' he said. 'You should really talk to her.'

He went out on to the veranda and called to Meredith, who was on her way back from the lemon tree. 'It's Lucy,' he said, wondering if he looked as bleak as he felt. 'For you.'

Meredith stiffened and Hal suddenly realised that he *did* look that bleak. She probably thought that Lucy had bad news. 'Don't worry,' he reassured her. 'Richard's fine.' He forced a smile. 'It's good news.'

Meredith hadn't been thinking about Richard, in fact. One look at Hal's face and she had known that the golden time was over and that everything was about to change.

Her heart was heavy as she picked up the phone. 'Lucy? It's me. What's happened?'

It was some time before she finally managed to say goodbye to Lucy and, by the time she did, Meredith was feeling completely numb. Very carefully, she put the receiver back in its cradle and went along to the kitchen, where Hal was waiting for her.

His grey eyes sharpened with concern at her expression. 'Are you OK?'

'I think so...yes...' But Meredith didn't sound too sure.

Hal tried a hearty smile. 'That was good news, wasn't it?'

'Lucy obviously told you.'

She needed to do *something* with her hands. For want of anything better, Meredith found the zester and started to zest the lemons she had picked.

'She said that Richard has realised that it's you he really wants.'

'Not exactly,' said Meredith quickly. 'She said she *thinks* I'm the one he really wants to see, but she doesn't know for sure. I gather Richard was quite embarrassed when he realised that Lucy had come all the way back from Australia for him. That was my fault,' she said with an edge of bitterness, putting one lemon aside and starting on the next.

Hal didn't know how to help her. 'It wasn't your fault, Meredith.'

'It was,' she insisted. 'I just assumed that was what he wanted and I made it happen. You were right,' she acknowledged dully. 'I should just let people get on with their own lives.'

'I'm glad you didn't,' he said. 'I wouldn't have met you otherwise.'

Meredith's hands stilled on the lemon. She glanced at him and then away. 'Lucy's sure that I'm still in love with Richard,' she confessed suddenly, 'but I really don't think I am.'

How could she be in love with Richard when she was in love with Hal?

She couldn't tell Hal that, of course. It would sound as if she wanted him to ask her to stay. And, if she did, Hal might even say yes, even though they both knew that it would end in disaster, no matter how much they might want to stay together now. They had different lives, different expectations, different futures.

Meredith couldn't even complain that this had come as a surprise. She had always known that this was going to happen sooner or later. The trouble was that she wasn't ready for it to happen just yet.

Some time in the hazy future, but not yet.

'Maybe when you see Richard again, you'll realise why you loved him before,' Hal suggested with difficulty.

'I hope so,' said Meredith, really wanting to believe it, but not quite convincing herself. She reached for another lemon and mustered a smile. 'I mean, Richard's perfect for me, isn't he?'

'You said once that he was everything you'd ever wanted.'

Everything *he* wasn't, Hal reminded himself. Richard was sensitive and artistic and cultured. He was a city man and Meredith was a city girl. He could offer Meredith the kind of life she was used to, the kind of life she wanted.

Hal thought about what Lucy had said. *She*

deserves to be happy. He wanted Meredith to be happy too, and the sick feeling in the pit of his stomach came from realising that Richard would make her happier than he could.

How could he promise her happiness when he knew how hard outback life could be, especially when he was—how was it she had put it?—a man with major commitment issues? Meredith was too important to him for him to start making promises that neither of them might be able to keep.

He swallowed. 'I promised Lucy I wouldn't stop you going home,' he told her. 'I told her I'd make sure you got the first flight possible.'

Meredith nodded without speaking. She was still zesting with a kind of desperation, but she stopped suddenly and stared from the lemon in her hand to the growing pile of bright yellow strips on the table before her.

'Oh, God, I don't need all this!' she exclaimed, only to find her voice breaking.

Pressing her lips tightly together in a perfectly straight line to stop her mouth wobbling, she scowled ferociously and willed herself not to cry. She never cried. She hadn't cried when her father had left her with Lucy all those years ago, and she wasn't about to start crying now. Crying wouldn't help.

Hal couldn't bear the look on her face. Stepping forward, he pulled her hard into his arms, where he didn't have to look into her eyes and he wasn't tempted to beg her to stay and make things even more difficult for her than they were already.

'Meredith,' he said, his mouth in her hair, breathing in the fresh, clean scent of her. 'Maybe this is for the best. You did love Richard,' he reminded her. 'Remember how you told me you were prepared to wait for someone perfect? You said you weren't prepared to settle for anything less, and Richard *was* perfect once. He probably will be again when you get back, especially now that he's come to his senses and realised what a special person you are.

'He can make you happy,' Hal went on raggedly, 'and I...I don't think I can.'

Meredith nodded wordlessly against his shoulder. She couldn't speak, couldn't do anything but hold on to him.

'I'll miss you,' he told her, his voice cracking. 'I'll miss you more than I can say, but there's no future for us. You know that.'

'I know,' she managed, muffled by his shirt, her arms around his back, clutching him. 'I know.'

'You're a city girl, and I live in the outback. If you stayed, you'd get bored, sooner or later, and then you would want to go.'

And you couldn't take being abandoned again, Meredith thought to herself. She couldn't take the risk of hurting him. She nodded again. 'I know, Hal. You're right.'

'Richard lives the same kind of life as you,' Hal went on, as if determined to prove to himself that saying goodbye was the right thing to do. 'You told me that you liked the same things. You both like music and food and going to Italy, all that kind of stuff. You'd miss all that eventually.'

'Yes, I probably would.' Meredith struggled to help him. She knew he was finding this as hard as she was. 'And we always said it was just a temporary thing, didn't we? That was what we both wanted.'

'Yes.' Just at that moment, Hal couldn't remember *why* he'd wanted it, but he knew that it was right.

'I just…don't know how I'm going to say goodbye to you,' she burst out.

Hal's arms tightened around her. 'It's going to be hard,' he acknowledged, 'but we were always going to have to say it some time.'

'You're right.'

Meredith pulled herself determinedly away from him and forced her wobbly mouth into an approximation of a smile. 'It looks like it's time to start being sensible again,' she said.

'That's my girl,' said Hal, although his throat felt so tight it was hard to get the words out.

'So…' She straightened her shoulders. The last thing Hal needed was her turning weepy and clingy at this point.

She found another smile, a better one this time. 'You go back to the yards and I'll make this cake, and then I'll find out about flights back to London. And we'll find a way to say goodbye when the time comes.'

CHAPTER TEN

'GOT everything?'

Meredith took a last look around the kitchen. She hadn't brought much with her, and she wasn't taking anything away. Except memories.

She picked up her laptop. 'Yes,' she said.

Hal had her case in one hand. He held open the screen door with the other and Meredith walked through it for the last time. Her shoes clicked on the wooden veranda and down the steps to where the truck was parked.

At the bottom she stopped and looked towards the creek where the ghost gums leaned, and then up at the tree where the galahs gathered. They were there now, huddled together along the branches in lines of pink and grey. It was very quiet.

Hal put her case in the back of the truck and, as if at a signal, the galahs erupted off the branches with much squawking and flurrying of feathers.

They took off into the brilliant blue sky in a blur of pink, turning as one so that their wings flashed silver in what might have been farewell.

Meredith's vision blurred as she got into the truck. *This is the last time,* she had been thinking ever since last night. The last time she would make love with Hal, the last time she'd lie against him and feel him breathing, the last time she would clutch at his hair and gasp his name. The last time she'd hear his boots on the steps, the last time she would see him put his hat on his head, the way he was doing right now.

Hal didn't speak as they drove down the track, and Meredith didn't look back. She sat staring straight ahead of her, concentrating on not crying, on just sitting there and breathing deeply.

On being sensible.

Hal was going to fly her into Whyman's Creek where she would pick up the plane to Darwin as Lucy had done, not so long before. Meredith had never been in such a small plane. It had four seats and a single propeller on its nose, but she was too wretched even to feel nervous, and Hal seemed to know what he was doing. He checked the controls, his eyes cool and calm, his fingers deft, and then the little plane was speeding down the runway, faster and faster, until it lifted into the air.

Meredith's stomach dipped as the ground dropped away beneath them. Had Lucy felt like this? she wondered. As if her heart were being torn out of her as the plane lifted into that immense sky?

Hal banked over the homestead and, as they turned, Meredith saw the corrugated iron roof flash in the sunlight. There was one last glimpse of the grey-green trees along the creek and then were they climbing, turning and climbing up into the blue. She craned her neck, suddenly desperate not to lose sight of it, but the homestead was already receding, growing smaller and smaller until it disappeared into the vast, featureless brown landscape and was gone.

They flew in silence. There was nothing to say. There was too much to say. You're being sensible, Meredith kept telling herself. It's the sensible thing to do. Just say goodbye and go.

Hal landed the plane at Whyman's Creek's tiny airport and taxied over to where several small planes like his were parked in a row. When he cut the engine and the propeller died, the silence was overwhelming.

Hal took a deep breath. 'Meredith—' he began, but she interrupted him.

'Wait!' she begged him. 'You don't need to say anything, Hal. In a moment, I'm going to get out and take my case and say goodbye. I'm going to get on the Darwin plane and I'm going to go home, and I'm not going to look back because we both know it's the right thing to do.'

She drew an unsteady breath and made herself go on. 'But…but I want you to know that the last few weeks have been the best of my life, and whatever happens there will always be a bit of me that still loves you the way I do now.'

Hal had turned in his seat to look at her and now he cupped her face between big, gentle palms. 'I love you too,' he said, very simply, because in the end, what else was there to say? They kissed, not a deep, passionate kiss, but one that was warm, tender, and heartbreakingly sweet, and Meredith's eyes were starry with tears when their lips parted at last.

'I won't ever forget you, Meredith,' Hal told her. 'I just wish …'

'That we weren't the people we are?' she finished for him as his voice trailed off hopelessly.

Losing the battle with a tear that spilled over her lashes, she wiped it away with a hurried finger.

He nodded. 'I wish we could do something about it, but we can't.'

'No.' Meredith took a deep, steadying breath. 'No, we can't.'

She gathered up her laptop. 'I think I'd better go, Hal. Don't come with me. I don't think I can bear it. Let's say goodbye here.'

So he simply lifted her case out of the plane and pulled up the handle so that she could trundle it along behind her. Meredith hoisted her laptop on to her shoulder and hesitated, holding her sunglasses in her hand.

'Actually,' she said, her voice high and cracked with strain, 'I don't think I'm going to be able to say goodbye.'

'Then we won't say it,' said Hal. His chest was so tight he could hardly breathe. 'Travel safely, Meredith. Be happy.'

She looked at him for one last moment, her vision swimming with unshed tears, and then she put on her sunglasses, took hold of her case blindly and walked away across the tarmac to the hut that passed as a terminal at Whyman's Creek.

Hal stood in the shade of the little plane and watched her disappear inside. A few minutes later the Darwin plane landed. It disgorged two passengers, and four more came out from the terminal and walked up the steps. Meredith's walk was so familiar to him by now that he could have spotted her even in a crowd.

He saw her hesitate at the bottom of the steps and glance his way, and he raised a hand to her. She lifted hers back and then went on up the steps and into the plane.

Come back! Hal wanted to shout.

He wanted to run over and pull her out, down the steps, back to Wirrindago, but the door was closing, the steps were being pushed back out of the way and the plane was taxiing to the end of the runway. It paused there for a moment and then launched itself forward, trundling faster and faster until, with a great heave, it lifted itself into the sky.

His heart like a stone in his chest, Hal watched it climb higher and higher into the glare until it was no more than a speck, and then even that vanished. Only then did he get back into the plane and fly home to Wirrindago.

* * *

Meredith tried. She really tried. She spent the long journey back to London telling herself that as soon as she got home, Hal and Wirrindago would be like a dream. It had only been a few weeks. How could it be more than a dream? It hadn't been *real*. It had just been a time out of time, when she had played at being someone else for a while.

The trouble was that it didn't feel like a dream. It felt all too real, and London was the place that seemed strange and unreal. The first morning that Meredith woke on her own to the subdued rumble of traffic rather than squabbling cockatoos, the longing for Hal and Wirrindago hit her with the force of a blow and she curled up in bed, hugging herself against the pain, biting hard on her lip to stop herself from crying.

She was hoping against hope that when she saw Richard all the old feelings would come flooding back and that her feelings for Hal would prove to be just a temporary obsession, a passing physical attraction, but sadly it didn't work that way. She was delighted to see him sitting up and talking, and felt real affection as she leant down to kiss him on the cheek, but love…no. She knew what love felt like now.

And, in spite of Lucy's certainty, Meredith was sure Richard felt the same. He greeted her like a good friend, and told her with much good-humoured rolling of the eyes how embarrassed he was that his parents had sent her off on wild goose chase, but she noticed that his eyes followed a rather pretty nurse who seemed to be finding all sorts of excuses to come into his room.

'So it looks like it was all for nothing,' Meredith confessed dully to Lucy later. 'I'm sorry. I should have left you alone in Australia.'

But then she wouldn't have known Hal. She would never have seen Wirrindago.

Lucy was bitterly disappointed when she discovered that Richard had resisted the opportunity to sweep Meredith into his arms and declare undying love.

'I was so *sure* that he was in love with you,' she said, sounding almost aggrieved. 'Once he'd confessed that he wasn't in love with me any more, he spent his whole time telling me how great you were, how easy you were to talk to, and how he hoped you'd come back soon.'

Meredith shook her head. 'Richard has only ever thought of me as a friend,' she said. 'He's never looked at me the way he used to look at you, or the way he looks at that blonde nurse.'

'Oh, her.' Lucy sniffed disapprovingly. 'She's always hanging around. I'm sure it's very unprofessional.'

'Maybe, but Richard looks quite happy about it.' Meredith smiled at her sister. 'To be honest, Lucy, I don't think he wants either of us!'

Lucy's face crumpled. 'I'm so sorry, Meredith. I've spoilt everything for you all over again! I should never have raised your hopes like that. I should have waited and found out exactly what the situation was instead of rushing in and getting it all wrong, the way I always do.'

She looked anxiously at Meredith. 'Are you very unhappy? You seem so sad.'

'I'm not unhappy about Richard, I promise you,' Meredith tried to reassure her. 'I'm just…'

Missing Hal. Wanting Hal. Needing Hal.

'…just tired,' she finished feebly. 'I'm still a bit jet lagged.'

'It takes a few days.' Lucy brightened, convinced at least that Meredith wasn't bitter about Richard. 'You must have been glad to get back to your nice house, though. You've been away for weeks.'

'Yes, it was time I came home,' Meredith agreed.

Only it didn't feel like home any more. Her cosy, comfortable house felt claustrophobic now. It was just a place without Hal.

She found a smile. 'Anyway, Hal said you could have your job back whenever you want.'

Lucy hesitated. 'I'm not going back, Meredith,' she said at last, and Meredith stared at her.

'But…I thought you loved it there! You told me you were in love with Kevin.'

'I know I did. I thought I *was*.' Lucy sighed. 'But…I think my feelings for him were just mixed up with how much I enjoyed being in Australia. I know the outback isn't your kind of place, but I found it all so romantic.'

It *is* my kind of place, Meredith wanted to shout at her. It is.

'But once I left,' Lucy went on, unaware of her sister's mental interruption, 'I started to think. Could I *really* spend my life somewhere like that? You know what an extrovert I've always been. Who would be my friends? I still think Kevin is incredibly attractive, but what would we have talked about after a while? The outback is all he knows, it's part of his charm, but I came to realise that I was being unrealistic.'

She glanced ruefully at her sister. 'I'm sure that's no news to you! You knew that all along, didn't you? You said you were sorry for coming out and making me leave Australia, but I'm glad that you did, Meredith. Otherwise I could have made a big mistake.

'It was me that made all the running with Kevin,' she said, 'and I could probably have swept him along into marriage, but what would he have done with a wife like me? I might not have been able to stick it out, and then I would have hurt him, and that would have been terrible. As it is, I bet he didn't really miss me that much, did he?'

'He seemed just the same,' Meredith had to admit.

Lucy's words resonated in her heart. *I could have made a big mistake... What would he have done with a wife like me?... I might not have been able to stick it out... I would have hurt him...* They could all apply to her, Meredith knew. She should be thinking like Lucy. Lucy thought that she would understand, and she did, but only with her head, not with her heart.

'It was just a holiday romance,' Lucy was saying. 'I realise that now, and some day I would like to go back to Australia, but not yet.'

'What about Hal?' asked Meredith, though it hurt just to say his name. Was that all their love had been? A holiday romance? 'He's been left without anyone to do the cooking.'

'I know, I feel bad about that,' said Lucy. 'But he said that they would be able to manage until he could find someone else. To be honest, I thought he might be more difficult about letting you go, but he was fine about it.'

Meredith thought about the way Hal had kissed her goodbye. *I love you,* he had said. He had let her go, but he hadn't been fine about it at all.

Drawing a breath, she forced a smile for her sister. 'So what now?'

'I've decided it's time for me to grow up,' said Lucy seriously. No more looking after me, Meredith. I've got to look after myself. I've got a job, and from now on I'm going to be sensible like you.'

Right. Sensible.

But being sensible didn't help. Sensibly, Meredith got straight back to work. Sensibly, she made sure that she went out with friends every night so that she didn't have too much time to think.

Sensibly, she reminded herself frequently that Hal didn't want any relationship to last longer than a few weeks or months. She told herself that he was right in saying that she would get bored of Wirrindago. After a month or two she would hankering for the bright lights. It was nonsense to suppose that she could be content with one man and a million acres of red earth.

And yet...and yet she couldn't stop thinking about Hal, about the last time he had kissed her. *I love you,* he had said, and she had believed him. They loved each other. She would be good for him, Meredith was sure. She could make him happy and she would be happy. They could have good life together, but how could she make him see that?

She couldn't force herself on him. Hal had said what he felt. He didn't want forever. We can't change the people we are, she had told him, but then, who *was* she? Was she careful, practical, sensible Meredith? Meredith who would never take a risk? Or was she a different person entirely?

She remembered how free and unfettered she had felt at Wirrindago. Jumping off that rock, sliding on to Hal's lap, loving him, she had discovered a sensuous side to her nature that she had never known before.

And it hadn't just been Hal's body. All her senses had been sharper there. She had been more *aware* of everything: of the smell of dried gum leaves in the creek, the sound of all those boots clattering up the steps to supper, the taste of billy tea, the feel of Hal's shirt brushing against her bare skin...

What if *that* was the real Meredith after all? Think about yourself, Hal had told her. What do you want? The trouble was that there were two answers. Her practical brain wanted to forget Wirrindago and get on with her life in London. It wanted to go back to the way she had been before—calm, content, not *yearning* for something more.

But her heart didn't want that. It wanted to feel that joyous sense of rightness again. It wanted to feel complete. It wanted to go home.

Doing the sensible thing would be safe. Following her heart would be a risk. A big risk.

Three weeks later, Meredith stared down from her bedroom window at the busy road, picturing a dry creek bed and a homestead with a lemon tree in the garden, seeing the galahs wheeling in the sky and a man in a hat walking up the veranda steps.

She knew what she wanted. Now the only question was whether she was brave enough to reach out and take it for herself.

'Wirrindago.' It was unmistakably Kevin's voice, and Meredith, who had been screwing up her courage for this moment for the past two weeks, didn't know whether to be relieved or disappointed. She had deliberately waited until lunchtime before ringing, but she had expected Hal himself to answer the phone.

'Hi, Kevin, it's Meredith,' she said, clearing her throat.

'Meredith!' Kevin exclaimed in surprise. 'We thought you'd gone back to the UK.'

'I did but…well, I'm back in Whyman's Creek. I'm ringing from the pub.'

'I hope you're coming back,' said Kevin. 'We haven't had a cook since you've been gone.'

'Who's been doing the cooking?' she asked.

'Hal, usually, but we're taking it in turns while he's away.'

'He's away?' Meredith stared at the phone in her hand. How could he not be there? Hal was always there. 'Where is he?'

'In Sydney.'

Sydney? It was the last thing Meredith had expected. In all the possible scenarios she had played out in her head, Hal being in Sydney simply hadn't occurred to her.

'He's gone to see his sister and the kids—hold on.' There was a murmured consultation in the background, then he obviously turned back to the phone. 'Ted says he's due back tomorrow. Do you want one of the guys here to come and fetch you this afternoon?' he asked hopefully.

'No, thanks, Kevin,' said Meredith slowly. 'I think I'll wait until tomorrow and see Hal here.'

Less embarrassing then if Hal said no to her proposition, she reasoned. Less awkward to catch the next plane back to Darwin and let her brain tell her heart *I told you so.*

But another twenty four hours to wonder if she was mad. What if he had just been *saying* that he loved her? What if he had met someone else? What if he was horrified to see her? What if…what if…?

Meredith paced restlessly around Whyman's Creek. It felt different this time, she thought, remembering how dismissive she had been of the little town. OK, it was no buzzing metropolis, but she liked the camaraderie in the shop, and she was happy to sit on the pub's veranda and watch the light and listen to the crows and think about Hal.

Bill was disappointed when she asked him if he would drive her out to the airport in time to meet the plane from Sydney the next day. His face fell. 'You're not going already?'

'One way or another,' she told him. She would be going somewhere, she just didn't know where yet.

Hal's little plane was parked where she had last seen it and Meredith waited for the Sydney flight to arrive in the shade of its wing. Sitting on her case, she was sick and shaky with nerves, torn between the longing to see Hal again and terror in case the greatest risk she had ever taken turned out to be the greatest mistake she had ever made.

With each minute that crawled past, the knot of anxiety inside her tightened and by the time the plane appeared Meredith had lost her nerve completely.

But she couldn't go back now. She had already jumped. It was too late to change her mind now.

She saw Hal as soon as he ducked out of the cabin and came down the steps and her heart, which had been thumping and thudding deafeningly ever since the plane had touched down, seemed to stop altogether. He only had hand luggage, so merely lifted a hand in greeting to the official waiting by the terminal and headed straight for his plane.

For her.

Slowly, Meredith stood up, ducking underneath the wing so that he would see her. When he did, he stopped dead, just like her heart had done.

'Hi,' she said in a high, cracked voice.

Hal took a breath and looked deliberately away from her, across the tarmac to the heat haze on the horizon, and then back. She was still there.

'Meredith…' he said, coming closer. He put down his case when they were face to face, his eyes never leaving her face, devouring her with his eyes. 'Meredith,' he said again, unable to find the words for the turmoil of emotion that he felt at the sight of her. 'It's you.'

'Yes.' She couldn't tear her gaze from his. It was as if they were having two conversations, and the one with their eyes was the only one that made sense.

Hal half shook his head, as if still not entirely convinced that he wasn't imagining things. 'What are you doing here?'

'I…um…I was hoping you'd give me a job,' she said. 'I understand you need a cook. Kevin sounds quite fed up.'

'You want to come back to Wirrindago?' Hal couldn't believe what he was hearing.

At last a question that she could answer with complete certainty. 'Yes,' she said. 'That's what I want.'

'Meredith…are you sure?'

'Yes,' she said again, and drew a deep breath. 'You told me once that I was afraid, Hal. You said I was afraid to reach out for what I wanted, but I'm reaching out now.'

Her eyes never left his. 'I know what I want,' she said. 'I want to be with you. I know you don't do forever, and I'm not asking for any commitment. I just need to be near you, for as long as I can.'

'But Meredith…' Hal felt uncharacteristically helpless. 'You can't give up your life in London.'

'I can,' she said. 'I *have* given it up.'

He was startled out of his numb sense of disbelief. 'You've done what?'

'I've given up that life. I've put my house on the market and I've applied to emigrate. I know you don't want to get married, Hal, and I can't be leaving every time my visa runs out.'

'But your friends…your career…' he said incredulously. Had she really done that? His sensible, practical Meredith?

'I've brought my career with me,' she said. It was the only safety net she had. 'I can work as well at Wirrindago as anywhere else. My friends can come and see me. And yes,' she said, 'maybe there *will* be times when I'll get bored. Maybe there will be times when I think I'd like to go and see a film or a concert or eat in a restaurant with white tablecloths and food I haven't cooked myself, but there's no reason why I can't take a trip to the city now and then, is there?'

'No,' Hal agreed.

'Well, then.'

A smile was dawning in Hal's eyes, warming them, spreading slowly over his face. He knew this Meredith, hiding her nervousness beneath that brisk veneer. She didn't fool him, though.

They still hadn't touched. 'And you've done all this without knowing what I would say?' he asked, and she nodded defiantly.

'I jumped. You were the one who taught me that I could,' she reminded him.

Hal took a step closer. 'This is a bigger risk than jumping off a rock.'

'I know,' she said. 'I know it isn't sensible, but I don't want to be sensible any more, Hal. I've changed,' she told him with a tremulous smile. 'I'm a risk taker now!'

'And you'll take a risk on me?'

The dark blue eyes steadied. 'On loving you, yes.'

'Even knowing that I've changed too?'

A chill ran through Meredith and she bit her lip. Was this the moment she had dreaded? Was Hal trying to tell her that he didn't love her the way he'd said he did before? Perhaps she had taken too much for granted. Perhaps she had jumped too far.

Swallowing, she put up her chin and made herself smile. 'If you've changed, you can say no and I'll go,' she said, knowing that he must be able to hear the tremor in her voice.

'Oh, no,' said Hal, and the smile reached his mouth as he pulled her into his arms at last. He didn't kiss her at first; he just held her tightly against him and felt her arms go round him, and they stood, hardly daring to believe that the waiting was over and they were holding each other again.

'I'm not going to say no,' he said against her hair. 'I'm not letting you leave me again. You're not the only one who's changed, Meredith. I'm going to be the sensible one from now on, and the sensible thing to do when you find the woman you want to spend the rest of your life with is to hold on to her, isn't it?'

Tipping her face up to his, he smiled down into her blue, beautiful eyes. 'In fact, the really sensible thing to do is to marry her.'

Her eyes widened in surprise. 'You don't want to get married!'

'I do now,' said Hal. 'I used to think that marriage had to be the marriage my parents had.

But then I started to think it didn't have to be like that. It could be being with you every day, holding you every night and waking up with you every morning. And I realised that was the marriage I wanted,' he told her. 'I wanted a marriage where you would always be there.'

His hands came up to cup her face and with one thumb he tenderly traced the line of her mouth. 'I missed you, Meredith,' he said, his voice deep and low. 'After you'd gone, I realised what a fool I'd been. The homestead was echoing without you. I couldn't go anywhere without expecting to see you, and then I'd remember you weren't there and I'd feel…bereft. I had a lot to say about how afraid you were, didn't I, but I was the one that was afraid. I was too afraid of losing you to let myself love you properly.'

They had both been afraid, thought Meredith. Her heart was so full she could hardly speak. 'Hal…' she said lovingly. She pulled him closer, her hands tightening possessively around him, giddy with relief that he was warm and solid and *there*. 'Don't be afraid.'

'I'm not now,' said Hal. 'Not now you're here.'

He kissed her then, and they clung together,

craving the reassurance of touch and taste. They couldn't hold each other close enough, kiss each other long enough, deeply enough, sweetly enough, and as the last shreds of uncertainty dissolved in the intoxicating rush, Meredith was filled with a deep gladness, fiercer than happiness, that burned up from the very core of her and told her that this time she had made the right decision and she was exactly where she was meant to be—in Hal's arms.

They smiled at each other when they broke apart at last, and Meredith rested her face into his throat with a sigh of sheer bliss. 'What made you change your mind?' she asked as his arms closed around her.

Hal kissed her hair. 'Missing you,' he replied. 'I kept going round in circles. I'd let myself imagine living at Wirrindago with you, having a family, you always being there...and then I thought about how it would feel if you left me the way my mother left and I knew I couldn't endure it, but I couldn't endure life *without* you either. I didn't know what to do, but I knew I had to do *something*. That's why I went to Sydney.'

'To see Lydia?'

'No, to see my mother.'

Startled, Meredith pulled back to look into his face. 'Your *mother*…?' Her eyes darkened with concern. 'That must have been difficult for you.' For both of them, she thought.

'It wasn't the easiest afternoon of my life,' Hal admitted. 'I kept wishing that you were there with me, but maybe it was something I had to do on my own. I should have done it before. When Lydia heard that I'd let you go back to London, she told me that I'd used our mother to justify my own fears for too long, and she was right.'

'What was it like, seeing your mother again after so long?' asked Meredith curiously.

'It was like meeting a stranger,' he told her. 'I thought I would be bitter and angry, but when I looked at her I just saw a woman who had made a mistake. She married someone she shouldn't have done and when she realised that she couldn't deal with it any longer, she left in the only way she could. Jack wouldn't have died if she hadn't gone, but it wasn't her fault. Or it was just as much my father's fault for not realising how unhappy he was,' he amended.

'It wasn't anybody's fault,' said Meredith,

resting her head back against his shoulder. 'Not your mother's, not your father's, not yours. It was something terrible that happened.'

Hal nodded, marvelling at how much better he felt just holding her in his arms. 'Anyway, I've realised that my mother is just one woman who has lived her life her own way, and that not all women are going to be like her. Lydia's not like her, *you're* not like her. You're Meredith, and I believe in you because of the person you are, and because I love you, and because I know that, whatever else might happen, you won't suddenly turn into my mother.'

Meredith tilted her face so that she could kiss the corner of his mouth with a smile. 'I'm glad.'

'Not as glad as I am to see you,' said Hal, his voice lightening. 'You've just saved me a lot of money.'

'I have?'

Not wanting to let her go, Hal kept one arm firmly around her and pulled a ticket out of his shirt pocket awkwardly with his free hand. 'I bought this in Sydney,' he said, 'but I should be able to get a refund now.'

Meredith opened it. 'It's to London!' She lifted

her eyes to his and her smile was dazzling. 'You were going to come and get me?'

'I was going to try and persuade you to come back. I didn't know if you'd be with Richard or not, but I knew that I had to try, I had to tell you how much I needed you, and that I was prepared to take a chance on the future if you were. Of course, that was before I knew how reckless you were,' he teased. 'I think I need a rather more sensible wife!'

Meredith smiled as she tucked the ticket back into his pocket. 'I expect I can still manage to be quite sensible about the little things,' she said. 'We just need to be brave about the things that matter, like trusting each other and loving each other,' she added with a soft kiss. 'Especially loving each other.'

'Are you sure?' Hal made himself ask, pulling her back hard against him. 'It can be a hard life.'

'I know,' she said. 'We'll have to work at it.'

'It'll be boring sometimes,' he warned.

'Maybe it will,' agreed Meredith, 'but I'm going to carry on my business, and there'll be the house to run and the chickens to feed and you to love, so I don't see that I'll have that much time to be bored. But if I am, I'll tell you, and we'll have a break together somewhere. I might miss being able to pop out for a cappuccino sometimes, but I can bear to miss it,' she said. 'I can't bear to miss you.'

'Meredith…' Hal kissed her, hoping that his kiss could tell her everything that words couldn't. 'You haven't said you'll marry me,' he said when he lifted his head at last.

'You haven't asked me,' she pointed out with a smile. 'Not properly.'

'Shall I go down on one knee?'

'No,' said Meredith. 'Just ask me.'

Hal smiled. 'I love you, Meredith. Will you marry me?'

'I love you too,' she said, tilting her face up to his, 'and yes, I will.

'This is all very nice,' she teased, emerging from his kiss some time later, 'but it's time somebody started being sensible round here. It's getting late.'

'That's true,' said Hal, tossing their cases up into the plane. 'We've missed your cooking, and I don't know if anyone's done anything about supper tonight.'

'In that case, you'd better take me home,' said Meredith and he cocked an eyebrow at her, smiling in a way that made her heart turn over.

'Home?'

'To Wirrindago,' she said and smiled. 'Home.'

MILLS & BOON PUBLISH EIGHT LARGE PRINT TITLES A MONTH. THESE ARE THE EIGHT TITLES FOR JANUARY 2008.

— ❦ —

BLACKMAILED INTO THE ITALIAN'S BED
Miranda Lee

THE GREEK TYCOON'S PREGNANT WIFE
Anne Mather

INNOCENT ON HER WEDDING NIGHT
Sara Craven

THE SPANISH DUKE'S VIRGIN BRIDE
Chantelle Shaw

PROMOTED: NANNY TO WIFE
Margaret Way

NEEDED: HER MR RIGHT
Barbara Hannay

OUTBACK BOSS, CITY BRIDE
Jessica Hart

THE BRIDAL CONTRACT
Susan Fox

MILLS & BOON
Pure reading pleasure

1207 Rom LP

MILLS & BOON PUBLISH EIGHT LARGE PRINT TITLES A MONTH. THESE ARE THE EIGHT TITLES FOR FEBRUARY 2008.

THE GREEK TYCOON'S VIRGIN WIFE
Helen Bianchin

ITALIAN BOSS, HOUSEKEEPER BRIDE
Sharon Kendrick

VIRGIN BOUGHT AND PAID FOR
Robyn Donald

THE ITALIAN BILLIONAIRE'S SECRET LOVE-CHILD
Cathy Williams

THE MEDITERRANEAN REBEL'S BRIDE
Lucy Gordon

FOUND: HER LONG-LOST HUSBAND
Jackie Braun

THE DUKE'S BABY
Rebecca Winters

MILLIONAIRE TO THE RESCUE
Ally Blake

MILLS & BOON®
Pure reading pleasure

0108 Ro